DEC 2019

P9-AZW-394

CARBON

Andrew Vachss

WITHDRAWN

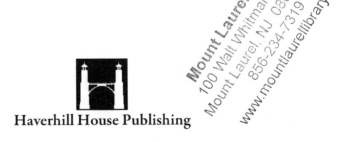

Haverhill House Publishing

Carbon
© 2019 Andrew Vachss

978-1-949140-13-2 Trade Hardcover
978-1-949140-17-0 Trade Paperback
978-1-949140-12-5 Limited edition Hardcover

First Edition

Haverhill House Publishing
643 E Broadway
Haverhill MA 01830-2420
www.haverhillhouse.com

Exit Music

When that last train leaves
with you its soul passenger
Who writes your obit?

For my brothers
　　　Ramón and Olaf.
Once blazing on two different sides of our earth,
　　now suns together in the same sky.

CARBON

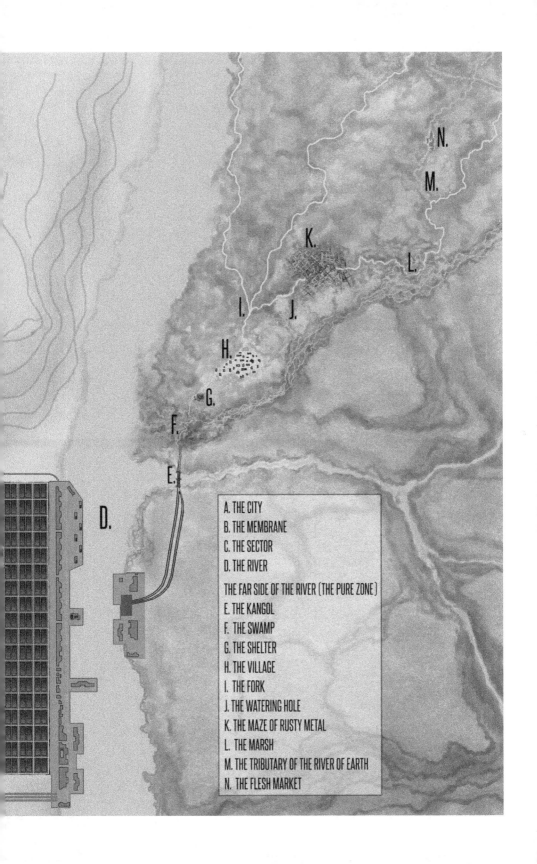

A. THE CITY

B. THE MEMBRANE

C. THE SECTOR

D. THE RIVER

THE FAR SIDE OF THE RIVER (THE PURE ZONE)

E. THE KANGOL

F. THE SWAMP

G. THE SHELTER

H. THE VILLAGE

I. THE FORK

J. THE WATERING HOLE

K. THE MAZE OF RUSTY METAL

L. THE MARSH

M. THE TRIBUTARY OF THE RIVER OF EARTH

N. THE FLESH MARKET

T. t's a law of life. When the people who got you out call you in, you're down to two choices: you come or you run.

The only place I could run to was the place I'd risked everything to leave.

A law of life isn't a written law, like the ones big thieves write for little thieves. It's a law like gravity. You can violate laws of life, but you can't break them. What breaks is always you.

So that's where it started. To be telling it true, *re-started.*

"I don't do that work," I told the featureless man carrying a titanium briefcase, keeping my voice soft. "Not for a long time, now."

"Not for seven years, seven months, and seven days. Some of that in Iso. All that did was make you harder, yes? Living up to your name. Again."

"You counted the time?" I said, not answering his not-

question.

"That was one of your qualifications."

"One?"

"You used to be the best at what you did," he said, nothing in his tone showing doubt. "Silence, that was part of what you did."

"I still do that part," I said, always mindful that manners show in both words and movement, letting the tone of my voice carry its true message. "You're so good at counting, no reason for you to stop now."

He shifted the briefcase slightly. "All right. We know you're not a talker, but that's not even in play anymore. My people don't require information from you—they just want to borrow your skills."

"You mean rent them."

"Say it anyway you like."

"Not planning a job? Nothing like that?"

"Nothing like that," he assured me, tilting his briefcase to deflect steel if he sensed it coming—whoever sent this one had done their research. "No planning. No going forward at all. What we need is a look into the past. The very recent past."

"I don't have a license anymore," I told him. "And I'm not getting it back. My deal was for a parole, not a pardon."

"There's a better deal on the table," he said. "There is

now, anyway," he went on, snapping open his briefcase. "That pardon's in the kitty, right in front of you. All you have to do is reach out and rake it in."

At next night, I was moving.

"Those cigarettes are all you have?" I asked the spring-coiled man whose knit tri-color tam was the only spot of color in his darkness. His blue-black skin reflected distant neon, and he was careful to never show his teeth.

"Yes," he said softly. "I'm only talking to you about this because ... you know."

"Say what you have to say," I told the undercover. I didn't need his explanations, just his information. And I knew he'd already been paid for that.

"All right, then. In the alley behind where it happened, the sweep team found three cigarettes, kicked underneath a wheeled metal dump bin. No identifiable bite marks on the filters, but they aspro-vac'ed enough DNA to test the first one."

"And that DNA traces to...?"

"Just the kind of slimy de-gen you'd expect."

"The cigarettes were his brand?"

"Don't know. Can't ask him. He's MOD."

"Missing or dead, sure. You have one of the untested

cigarettes with you?"

"I do. But if I ever got caught handing it over to a...."

"I'm not the one to talk to about protection."

"But you can talk to them, yes? Tell them I'm—"

"—No, I can't. I'm a hired man, working a contract. A new contract. So I'm *from* them, not *of* them. You want me to learn anything from that cigarette, I have to take it apart. You want to talk to other people first, your choice."

"I have to make a phone call."

"Don't."

"Don't what?"

"Don't be that stupid."

"Look, friend, it's not your life, here."

"No, it's not. But if you use a phone to make yourself feel better, it could be *yours*."

"You know who I am, and yet you threaten me?"

"All I'm doing is telling you the truth. Your line of work, you don't see that too often, do you? So you should recognize it when it shows up."

First, I slathered my hands in the fingerprint-scramble solution, then carefully laid the cigarette on a small pane of acid-washed glass. I worked the surgical scalpel carefully, cutting so shallowly that the paper wrapper

seemed to separate itself.

There were two loads past the filter. Different grits to the touch. Different smells, too. Fresh sniffs different than stale.

"You don't know what brand the MOD smoked?" I asked the no-longer undercover. The same question I'd asked him before, expecting a different answer this time.

"Loosies," the cop said, proving me right.

"Then this one, it should be a different brand than the one your team already opened. And the one still intact, too. All three, different."

"How can you be so sure?" he asked. Not a challenge, really wanting to know.

"This cigarette here? It's been hand-loaded. Expensive trick. Tobacco, that's a plant you grow. But this construction, it's a plant you *plant*. And what's inside a plant? A seed, right? Like in that old Bob Marley song: 'Kill it before it grows.' That kind of seed."

"You think you can play color games with me, mahn? I should know Bob Marley because, what? My accent? This tam? My dreds? I can play that way, too, I want. You are no mystery to me. I know your ink, right down to those 88s on your triceps. No need to take off your shirt—it's all in your file."

"From that, you know me?"

"I know enough, don't I, now?"

"No. No, you don't. You have my prints, sure. Mug shots, dental charts, stuff like that. Might help you ID my body, but doesn't tell you my mind."

"I know a bit more than that," he said, confidence flowing smooth. "You were gift-wrapped a seven-to-twenty-one plea on two bodies. And you only got one little six-month tap from the Board before you gated. For a deal that sweet, you must have closed a lot of cases."

"Cases. Not people. Whatever I said, it was just paper-talk."

"On *your* paper, it says a lot of things, maybe."

"Sure. Says I shouldn't have been paroled at all, yes?"

"It does say that. And like *you* say, you cleared the books on a lot of stuff. Old stuff. Old *cold* stuff. And you skated quick over that thin ice."

"I did. So, the parole I shouldn't have gotten, that tell you anything?"

"Time's short for games, mahn."

"I didn't deal this hand. Anytime you want to pass, call your shot. I know why I was sprung. Found out real quick. Got that contract memorized. If you knew me like you say, you'd know I keep my word. Always. So let's get to it, okay? The seed-killer in Marley's song, that was the Sheriff."

"A *white* sheriff. But I carry the same badge he did. Want me to show you?"

"I've seen it."

"Badges? You must have seen a lot of them."

"*Your* badge. D-29977."

"Where did you see that?" he said, unable to keep his voice flat, self-assurance oozing away like sap from a spike-tapped tree. "They wouldn't let you near those files."

"On your night stand. Teak, with a purple heartwood streak laid in. One on each side of the bed."

"You saw that?" he said, voice tightening. "Or you saw a picture?"

"That," I lied.

"So.... Another threat?"

"No. Another piece of truth," I told him.

"You want some truth, try this on, then: I'm not playing this for money."

"I know that."

"You *know?* How could you—"

"Not all files are in computer banks. And my files show more than yours do. I just proved that, didn't I?"

"Prove some more, then."

"One more try," I told him, adding "last one," as an underscore. "You're not playing for money, but if you *hadn't* asked for money, the people who reached out to you would have known more than they should. More about you."

"What *you* know, you're saying? More from those

'files' of yours?"

"What I know I keep to myself. What I know of the living, *that's* what I'm saying. You looked at my record, you already know that. Just be calm, just listen, and I'll tell you what I know. About this, I mean. I'll tell you because the people who paid me don't care *how* it happens, understand? Only that it does."

He nodded, as mutely speechless as if I were wearing a body mic.

"A cigarette like this one, it has to be engineered," I told him. "The killer—the real killer, not the distracts, those MODs—the killer could have just picked up a few random butts anywhere, but that wouldn't target anyone specific ... especially if they all came up DNA-different. This cigarette here is one meticulous piece of work. Extracting the unsmoked tobacco without tearing the paper, then sandwiching the new infusion between the filter and the stale stuff behind the burnt end of the tip...."

"Sounds like a work no one needed to bother with," the cop said. "The MOD, he was a smoker—it's in his file. Why not snatch him, let him smoke a few while you're keeping him quiet, then just make him disappear?"

"Disappear doesn't work," I told him. "Wouldn't look

good, would it? He vanishes, that reads like your manhunt flopped. And an arrest wouldn't solve your problem either, no matter how tight you built the frame. What if the distract's got an ironclad for when it happened? You never know with a de-gen, do you? He could have been hospitalized for weeks, locked up for a night, or even on some dupe's Tracebook page exposing himself ... you couldn't ever be sure. Not a hundred percent. In a game like this, if you can't be *that* sure, you don't even ante. The MOD, the distract—it's not as if he was under surveillance before the killing, right?"

"Registered sex offender."

"Like I said."

"Okay, so nobody was actually keeping tabs on him. Not that close, anyway. So what?"

"So DNA isn't date-coded," I told him. "The tobacco in the cigarettes is still another misdirect." Time for me to play a higher card: "The DNA you pulled from the filter, that's not the same as the tobacco inside, is it?"

"How could you...? No. No, it wasn't."

"And that traced, too, didn't it? To *another* MOD. With the same kind of sex jacket. Two maggots out on the stalk, sharing a smoke, working each other up. A nice bonding ritual. Helps with the nerves, too. So they were waiting, watching a bedroom window for lights to go out. Her apartment was third floor rear, just across the alley

from that dump bin."

"They didn't have the same jackets. But close, anyway."

"So this wasn't a brand-name loosie at all. It was a roll-your-own."

He took a half-step back. Looked at me closely, as if reading a translation from a foreign language. "You are either very good, or...."

"There's no other source," I finished his sentence. "None possible. You're the only one working the case they reached out to," I told him, not asking. I was pushing hard—pushing *against* his fears. No need to spell out who "they" were. Or that I was standing between them and him.

"You're not a payroll guy," I said, gently. "They came to you only because you caught the case. That's why you asked for money, so they wouldn't spook. And, me, if you actually believe anything in my file, you already know I'm a wrong number for your calculator."

"Bring the rest of it, mahn," he said quietly, gesturing like a fighter who just took a hard shot, smiling as he waved the other man in. Come closer and try your luck.

I took the offer. "There's machines that can roll cigarettes from scratch, filter and all. Haven't seen them around for a while, but you can still find them in the Sector. Or you could make one easy enough.

"And there's plenty in that very business," I followed

up. "They collect discards: nightclub ashtrays, smoking patios, alleys where they have blanket dice games.... Easy after that: tear the discards open, pile the tobacco, razor the filters down just enough to look new."

"You're saying there's money in that? Building new smokes from butts?"

"How could there not be? The tax on cigarettes is so high that smuggling is a big-money racket, now. Loosies are a trey apiece, minimum. Making them up from discards is labor-intensive, sure ... but labor's cheap if it's not paper-cleared to work."

"You're making it sound like a damn spy movie. Why would anyone build smokes with mixed tobacco? And then plant them?"

"Come on, think like a cop," I pushed him. "One degen goes MOD right after that killing, everyone figures he panicked and ran. *Two* go the same time, it figures that if they teamed up to do the job, maybe they'd run together, too."

"The other one wasn't a rapist. He was—"

"—A pyro."

"Good guess. And he was a peeper, too. On the Registry for it."

"Nice package, then. Your people can probably put them together before the fire?"

"Already did. Self-help group. Called RPFC. "Re-

Programming False Cognitions."

"Somebody else put them together, too."

"The killer, you're saying. So you think they're both gone."

"Atomized," I assured him.

"And you got all that off one loaded cigarette?"

"I got more." I promised, speaking as if his sarcasm had been praise. "There's a kind of forensics you won't see on those stupid TV shows, and you don't need microscopes to put it in play. I've read all the files—the same ones you have. The woman's building was three-star. That means central air, but her windows were open. In ninety-plus heat? Sure.

"Ventilation is a better accelerant than gasoline. And, yeah, some de-gens love fire for its own sake, but it's still the ultimate evidence-wipe. That cigarette told the true story: this was a professional at work, all right. But not a torch—a hitman."

"If it's like you say, misdirection, you're also saying this wasn't a sex crime?"

"Much too subtle for that. That fire, it wouldn't burn long enough to turn bone into ash. So the killer would know you were going to ID the body sooner or later. The Arson Squad is good this side of the Membrane. Good enough to set up a perimeter, go poking around outside the burn scene. And somebody knew that, too."

"Anyone could know that."

"Sure. Especially a convicted pyro, you'd think. Just like you were *supposed* to think," I told him, thinking of the flame-freaks I'd talked with over the years. Especially one I'd done time with. He was a strange man, even for that place.

"It's not the look of it," he told me one night, after the count. *"Not the flames. That's what people think, but they don't know. They don't understand. It's the sound. Fire has its own sound. A special sound. Not everyone can hear it call. But once you do...."*

"So what now?" the undercover asked. As if we'd teamed up, me in the lead, him waiting for instructions.

"Now you tell me everything you know about—"

"—I gave you what I had," he said, shifting his stance slightly. "There is no more."

"Not about forensics, about the victim," I said, finishing what he'd interrupted. "Not just what you have now, whatever you can put together. Go back as far as you can."

This side of the Membrane, night doesn't just show up. It descends like a slowly draping shroud. My eyes penetrate the darkness from what the City maps show as a

no-access roof. I sweep over costumes, slide past poses, practicing my patience as trailing ribbons of car headlights bounce jaggedly off icy neon-swirling signage.

An anaconda of menace prowls the ground fog, a thick vein visible only by its erratic pulse, mindless until genetic propulsion kicks in. But this beast can't gobble its kills— the only option on its menu is slow-consume. Vulnerable after it kills, until it finds a safe place to turn prey into nourishment.

The same place it left to hunt.

I will watch relentlessly until I learn that place. Once I know, once I'm *sure,* then it's all down to timing the strike.

It's not just that I never talk; I'm never curious, either. But if I wake up and the streets are wet, I know it probably rained while I was asleep.

Somebody murdered a working girl and DNA-fingered a couple of de-gens for it. Not a rage-kill, not with how much work went into it. There's as many reasons for killing as there are killers. What the news-feed always calls a "senseless crime" only has to make sense to whoever committed it.

The people who hired me wanted the killer. They

didn't want him killed. Not even captured. They just wanted to know who he was.

The people who hired me are the ones who got my sentence cut. The same ones who got the undercover to talk to me. There's law, and there's law enforcement. And there's those who live past where either can touch.

I couldn't figure their math, but I wasn't getting paid to do that.

Three nights later. The diner had a booth set flush against its back wall. And in front of that booth, two empties. Always two empties.

"She was in the Life some kind of way, but we couldn't find a back-trail."

"You think ... what?" I asked the undercover.

"Nothing *to* think, mahn. Expensive building, like you said, but she'd only been there a couple of months—the place was barely furnished. And she'd been out of the hospital for just a little longer than that."

"Hospital for...?"

"All kinds of surgery. She was admitted after a car crash. Her car, but the auto-drive had been remotely accessed by a hacker. Straight into a construction site at a good speed, no brake application. She should have been

killed."

That's why the Government gives a damn. A killing is a killing. Those happen. But a hacker who can re-direct an auto-drive might be capable of a total system disruption. Flirting with the border of Intolerable.

"Before that?"

"Straight-line, straight-edge. She was twenty-seven, college graduate, Government job, but nothing sensitive. Always lived well above her salary, but no evidence of dealing, no contraband ... and no sugar daddy."

"You have photos?"

"Before and after, mahn."

I worked him for nearly an hour, thinking I wouldn't get another chance.

We didn't part friends. But we shared an understanding.

Some trackers work in all-black, but a passing prowl car could cause that to *pop* in those blue stack-laser headlights they run. So when I'm doing this work, I dress in black-and-gray random splatter, back alley camo.

All private cars are programmed; they self-drive to whatever destination the owner punches in. And that same info goes right into the City databank. Only police

cars are operator-driven.

I watched as my target OCD-tapped the rust-blotched door eight times, keeping my pulse slowed at the resting state I'd been holding for over an hour. The target knew the territory, knew this part of the City was as **PELIGROSO!** as its graffiti claimed. And I knew him. Knew he couldn't pass a chalk-marked door without his stylized tapping. Not to get in. Not to let anyone on the other side know he was there, never that. His taps were a ritualized placation to the only god he knew. But that night, I was the only one listening.

"Don't get excited," I whispered behind him. "And don't get stupid."

"Are you...?"

"Ssshh. I'm the man you came here to meet."

"How do I—"

"—I asked you not to be stupid. I was anyone else, you'd be bleeding out by now."

"I ... I can't talk here."

"Here's all there is."

"Can I turn around?"

"You *want* to see my face?"

"Listen," he whispered. "Yeah, I went in there to steal,

okay? To ... take stuff, you know? Just like always. That's me. That's what I do. But once I saw her, saw how they'd left her, I knew I couldn't take nothing."

"But you *left* something?"

"No! I'm a pro ... give me that much. I went in clean, like always. But when I saw that...." He made some sound only he could understand. "I knew I couldn't take nothing, not even the cash on the dresser."

"How long ago?"

"A couple of hours, no more."

"You made a lot of calls fast."

"Just the one."

"They told you the price?"

"Yeah. But it wasn't my fault. It wasn't me who ... did that to her. And, I told you, I didn't take anything from the place. Why should I be the one to pay?"

"Ask whoever you called. But I don't have time to get into arguments with you. If you want it done, it has to be quick."

"I don't have that kind of coin. Not on me, I mean. But I can get it for you. Just give me...."

"This is Tuesday night. Call whoever you called. Tell them you'll have the money in forty-eight, no longer. Tell them where to pick it up."

"How do I know you'll—"

"—Listen for the fire sirens," I told him.

He was the third one. And he hadn't been surprised that I could order a fire to cover whatever horror-show display he'd found in that apartment. But he wasn't the one I was looking for. That one, he wouldn't have made a call. Not to anyone, not ever. And he'd know how to strike his own matches.

"There's a glass ceiling in your business," I told the woman, watching her silverfish eyes try to slide past mine. She had a classic oval face and *café au lait* skin, black lipstick slam-contrasting against braided hair the color of dried blood.

I told her that after we'd finished. After I'd finished, anyway.

"I used to hear that 'glass ceiling' thing a lot," she said, lighting another Thai stick. "From girls who came to the club for those stupid bachelorette parties. But I don't understand what it's supposed to mean."

"It's like being a non-violent drug dealer. You can look up all you want, there's a nice clear view. You can *look* up; you can *see* up ... but you can't *move* up. Not unless you—"

"The only time *I* look up is when—"

"—Save it. You know who sent me."

"Actually, I don't. I only—"

"—You're too smart a girl to be talking this much."

"Then I'll be quiet."

"Where you are, there *is* no 'up,' okay?"

"And no 'out,' either."

"That part's not true."

"You know where the exit is? *You?*"

"Better," I promised. "I've got the key to it."

"How do I know you're not just—"

"—Because I only tell the truth."

"Sure."

"Here's some more of that truth: A friend of yours, there was a fire in her building. Not a big one, but more than enough to finish her, trapped in her apartment like she was. Probably drunk. Or soft-buzzed ... like you are right now. Probably never knew the place was on fire until it was too late. Or maybe she never woke up at all."

"I don't know any—"

"—Layne. Layne Violette. Her work name. Layne like Jayne with an 'L.' If that doesn't jog your memory, try 'Zelle.' Or 'Mai Zelle.' Half Chinese. Half at least. The other half mixed."

"Oh god! You're one of those...." she whispered, staring at the ink on my torso, the ink that hadn't made

any difference before I'd let words like "race" and "mixed" into my mouth.

"For you, I'm not."

"Because I'm...?"

"Aryan? No, you're not. I know you're not. But that's not in play. I said what I said only so you'd know *I* know. So you wouldn't have to waste time pretending that you never knew that girl."

"Okay, I knew her. But we weren't—"

"—Stop," I said. Very quietly, but not in a whisper. "Here's what I need: clients. Layne Violette's book is gone in the fire, but she'd have a backup. And she'd keep it with a friend."

"I don't—"

"—Yeah, you do. She was your roommate, once. Did the same work, starting out. But while she was in the hospital, you moved away. And she moved up. Closer to that ceiling. But you stayed close."

"Oh god. You think it was one of Mai's—"

"—Yes. I found you, so other people can find you, too. So give me that book of hers, now. Yours, too. You won't need it anymore, not once you go through the exit."

Then I crossed the Membrane again.

The kid watched as his model airplane crashed. He was straddling puberty—too old to burst into tears, but still young enough that he had to tighten his face against it.

I picked up the plane as he ran over with his father. When the kid got close enough to see what I was doing, I took a roll of black gloss duct tape from my coat.

"Are you going to tape the wing back together?" he asked me.

For answer, I broke the other wing.

Now the kid was straddling another border: run at me, or run away.

"If we just tape one side, it won't balance," I told him, handing the body of the plane to his father.

I flicked out my tanto. Then I unfurled a strip of tape. "Hold this end," I told him, as I slashed off four strips and touched them to the sleeve of his jacket.

"Now hold the pieces together," I told the father. "Carefully. They have to fit. Don't force it."

I taped the wings, just the undersides first, then a full wrap so each wing was equal.

His father spun the propeller. The engine caught.

The plane taxied cleanly. Then it took off.

While the kid joyfully worked the controls, I asked the father some questions.

My kind of work doesn't have a fixed rate. Not even a guaranteed one—sometimes, you end up working for nothing. I worked the model airplane kid's father for over an hour, and all I got was the name of a trouble bar on the other side of the Membrane.

Not new info to me. I even knew the guy who pulled the taps at that joint. He was a master mixologist—anytime he served up a dose of the truth, it always came with a twist.

Ask him where to find someone, he'd tell you. Then he'd tell them. An evolved parasite, he only sucked blood from the juiciest part of the middle.

Absolutely reliable, he was. You could count on him to betray someone ... you could just never be sure who. That was what kept him alive all these years. He was too fat to run, but you wouldn't want to be on the wrong side of him if he fell.

He understood a half-dozen languages, including sign, but he would never speak any of them, only listen. The way it worked, if you ordered a beer, you had something to sell. Hard stuff meant you wanted to buy. Ordering a mixed drink meant you'd wandered in by accident. If he knew your face, he'd put a glass of water in front of you.

Mine came with ice—he knew the kind of work I did.

The fat man never left the bar. No one had ever seen him outside. Why would he ever need to leave his planted spot? In the Sector, you could get anything delivered ... even the delivery boy.

The bartender had once put me together with a fringe-working City lawyer who needed something done. That was a long time ago, back when I had a license.

A rich woman's son was in jail, awaiting trial. She had all the money, but that wouldn't cure the remand. The charge sheet was too heavy for any bail to lift: stalking, sexual assault, terroristic threats, carrying concealed.

"He's a sniveling little wannabe," the lawyer said of his client. "Dresses like a movie gangster, talks about his 'boys'... of which there aren't any. He's got a pistol permit, but it's target-range only. The full-carry's pending, but could the punk manage *not* to walk around 'strapped' until we made him legit? Oh *hell* no."

"And my job would be ... what?"

"Not what you think," the lawyer said. "Look, there's no budget on this one, hear what I'm saying? Mommy's got assets, and she's going the limit—it's her money that's keeping him safe in lockup. Now, on those charges, there's

one we can work with: the damn pistol *was* registered, so he was carrying it to the range, okay? The other's got an opening, too. The punk paid some banger he met in lockup. The banger got one of his mob to call the vic's phone and tell her what would happen to her face if she testified. Naturally, she recorded the call, everyone does that now. But it wasn't our boy on the line, so there's some room to maneuver there, too. Even if the DA flips the banger, his kind don't carry their cred in front of juries."

"That leaves the rape."

"Sexual assault."

"Whatever you call it."

"You ready for this? He's innocent."

"Okay."

"Don't 'okay' me, friend. When you've got enough money, you can buy people, sure. But, sometimes, you can buy something better."

"Better than people?"

"Much better. Truth, that's what's better. You know how often a man in my business gets a for-a-fact innocent client who's also a paying customer? That's *gold*. Pure gold."

"Gold fluctuates."

"It does. But this—right here, right now—this is priceless."

"You're going to say what you want sooner or later,

right?"

He gave me a look. Stopped short of lighting his green-banded cigar, settled for a cigarette he took from a small humidor. Didn't offer me one.

"First of all, that stalking charge: it's fairy dust. On that, they got nothing. On the sexual assault ... okay, here's where you listen. That woman—the so-called 'victim' here—she's a stone psycho. Gets her kicks riding the trains, picking out the right patsies, crying rape."

"You know this ... how?"

"Because she's done it three times already! Three times *before* this. Always the same exact script. She pulls at her blouse, plays under her skirt, lures the sucker close ... and then starts screaming. Everybody on the train gets to be a hero: some pile on, some work their phone cameras, some actually use the phones to call the cops. She works the role perfect."

"So those other cases, what happened?"

"Always the same thing. She collapses. They hospitalize her. PTSD. Rape Trauma Syndrome, all that. Victim Services says she's too fragile to testify. When she collapses, so do the cases. Sooner or later, they all go away. Except...."

"Except one of the mopes pleads out, yes?"

"How did you— Ah, never mind, I know your rep. Actually, *two* of them pleaded. Now you're going to tell

me why, right?"

"Wants and warrants. Other charges pending. A roll-up. Total package deal. Or maybe your info isn't so good. Maybe the woman's a nut-case, but nut-cases can still get raped."

"No. The info's good," he said, every word dripping assurance.

"Because a couple of—"

"—Because she told the psychiatrist!" he came with, almost vibrating over his trump card. "Told the psychiatrist the truth, I'm saying. While she was hospitalized. Look, who knows what gets a rapist's rocks off? We know it isn't sex, but all the rest is just guesses ... mostly political ones at that. But screaming 'Rape!'—being the poor victim, heroically fighting off an attacker—that's what gets *her* off."

"And a psychiatrist ... the psychiatrist who treated her, not some whore you hired, he told you that?"

"She."

"What?"

"She. Her psychiatrist in the hospital was a woman. And we got the whole report. This so-called 'victim,' she's as loony as they come. 'Munchausen syndrome with fragment mutation,' that's the diagnosis. You know what that means?"

"Like when someone poisons themselves so they keep

going to the hospital? Or gets all kinds of surgeries they don't need?"

"That's right. And all for the attention. Some of them even poison their own kids. For the same reason."

"You got all that on paper?"

"Every word. And, yes, I know ... we can't show it in court. Never mind the whole 'confidentiality' thing; it's also a privileged communication, no way it gets in. But we can still use it."

"That means, the victim, she's out of the hospital now?"

"You guessed it. And you see how we can use that report, yes? Or do I have to spell *that* out for you, too?"

"He's been *stalking* me!" the woman spasm-sobbed, pointing a long pink fingernail at me. I didn't move from where I was lying on the floor of the commuter train.

She wasn't lying about the stalking part. I'd been her shadow for that whole week—a shadow she'd thrown a few little wiggles at, pulling me in.

"I'm a Cross-Membrane PI," I told the two uniforms who cuffed me up. "My license's in my wallet."

"What's that mean, you're not gonna invoke?" one of them sneered.

"I'm working a job," I said, calmly. "She's a fraud. Pulled the same number before. There's a business card next to my license. A lawyer. The lawyer for the guy who's locked up. He's the one who hired me."

"It's a good story," the other cop said. "You can tell it to the detectives. Unless you're saying that lawyer's card means you invoked...."

"If you didn't grope under her skirt, how'd her panties get ripped?" the younger detective asked. More a polite question than a snarl. So he was unsure of his ground—maybe someone had already made a call.

"I can't tell you that," I told him. "I *can* tell you I didn't touch her at all, never mind grope her."

"We've got your phone," the older detective said, softly. "But we're not thick enough to look at it. Not yet. We're waiting for the warrant. And we both know what we're gonna find on that phone, don't we? Come on, don't make it worse than it is. A little upskirt action, you know that's nothing more than a dis-con when your lawyer gets through with it."

"It's not my phone you want to look at," I told him.

"Who's then? Hers?"

"No. My operative's. The Spanish kid I brought with

me from the agency. He was in the crowd. You questioned him, but you didn't ask the right ones. He's got the whole thing on tape. Audio and video."

Soon as they were finished, so was my contract.

But all that kind of work was before I'd gone in. Before I chased a change-it-all score all the way down to Hell.

Now I was back to working contracts. I opened by making sure the fat man behind the bar understood a few things. I was back. Not an escapee, a free man. The leash was none of his business. All he needed to know was that I was doing whatever I'd done before I'd gone away. He was never sure of my game, but he always knew the stakes I played for.

He nodded, not meeting my eyes. I told him what I needed.

When you're on the run, no illusion of safety ever lasts long. Even if you don't recognize any of the faces that cross your visuals, what's that worth? The upside is nobody knows you—the downside is you don't know anyone. Hunters would be locals, working with fine-grain photos supplied by their paymaster. You wouldn't

recognize them. So you'd never see them coming.

Here, the script was flipped. I didn't have the killer's face, true, but he didn't have mine, either. I knew he wasn't a stranger to the Sector. In this cesspool, he'd have to be a native fish to have done all the work that was already down to him on the other side of the Membrane. So this is where he'd come to hide out.

I wouldn't know him if I saw him. But if I crossed his path too many times while I was looking, he'd know me. So I worked the path he'd already marked. I couldn't tell you his face, but I knew his work, knew he was cold enough to flow through ice. So I started where the temperature never rises high enough to please a reptile.

All those years of working cross-Membrane had imprinted a City map on my brain. People might have changed since I'd gone in, but not districts. So I knew where to start.

Maybe I wasn't Central Casting for Irish, but shamrocks were part of my ink. And green's universal for money. So I was good enough for the next joint.

"Michael," he said, introducing himself, holding out his hand for me to test. "Michael Hennessey."

"White," I said, limp-gripping him so he'd know I

wasn't about meaningless measurements. "Carbon White."

"What kind of name is that?"

"Mine."

"'White,' is it? Lot of coloreds are named that. You wouldn't think so, maybe, but it's true. And 'Carbon,' that's black, too."

"Try them together," I told him. "And names don't mean much, anyway, do they? Take 'Michael,' that's a Jew name, isn't it?"

"What?" Not a question, a hostile demand.

"In your book, Michael the Archangel, he's the patron saint of soldiers. In theirs, he's an archangel, too. Jews, they don't have saints."

"Not many would know that. Any of that."

"Less would care," I answered, using his same code.

"You know why they call this place 'church?'" the short, powerfully built man with no-iris blue eyes finally said.

"Because it's holy ground?" I ventured.

"Ah, that's not bad. And maybe it's close. But, close, that wouldn't be describing you and me, would it?"

"No."

"Still, I know your name. And you've got a good word on you. Been a while since I heard that, but I've not heard anything to the contrary since. Unusual, that. Seems like

more so every day."

"Color doesn't tell you everything, does it? Grass, that's green."

"That it is. Although not when it's burnt, aye? But, like I said, I've not heard of you in some time."

"I've been away."

"I've been away myself, in the past. Not in this blessed country, but to the same place, I think."

"Yes."

"So. You're a buyer? Or a seller?"

"Buyer, I hope. Prospective, for certain."

"Don't say anything to me. Not a word more, mind. I'll be leaving now. The lady who'll be sitting across from you soon, she'll listen. And maybe ... I say, *maybe* now, she'll tell you where you might run across word in a day or two."

It was three days.

I watched the blocky man wearing a black felt hat cross the street toward me. If the misty rain bothered him, he gave no sign.

"That's a beautiful old church," I said, looking past him over his shoulder.

He didn't turn his head. "It is that. I go whenever I feel the need."

"Confession?"

"Confession isn't part of my religion, son."

"It's a Catholic church."

"Of course it is," he said, as if there were no other kind. "But confession, that's for a sinner who seeks forgiveness. And, me, I don't qualify."

Then he told me what I'd offered to pay for.

My ink had been an investment. I'd invested my patience, too. Not all of it, but edge-close to the margin. Waited years before I moved.

That's the rule of patience. I learned it as a child. By listening. "It's ten o'clock now, boy. If you wish for it to be nine, your wish can't come true. But if you wish for it to be eleven, all you have to do is wait."

I had time, I kept telling myself. Ended up doing it.

The money had been stolen before I was born. Six separate armored car hits. Eleven bodies, all guards. Five more scores in separate bank takedowns. Bloodless, those last ones—by then, the whole City knew the robbers would slaughter any who resisted them.

None of the money was ever recovered. Some whispered it was poisoned: bang-dyed orange, impossible to circulate. Others said it had been washed through a

network of overseas banks. Croatia was the country most mentioned, but Estonia was on that list, too. I'd never been to any of those places, just knew the names. Didn't even know if they really existed. But the money, *that* I knew was real.

And, rumors be damned, I knew it hadn't been touched. All that money had been meant to finance a plan called "Dark White." Those of pure genes were going to take over and rule the City.

The Dark White plan had never included the Sector. There, only small pieces of territory could be held, and never for long. Take over the Sector? Impossible. Even the thought was madness. The Pure Zone was out, too—it was so vast it had never been charted, so disconnected it could never be conquered.

The Sector was high-tech primitive. It held people so compressed that even oxygen sometimes ran short. The Pure Zone was a surplus of everything, but a total absence of technology ... a wild place where sorcery worked but firearms did not.

But the City, that was there for the taking. The City with its fatal structural flaw ... a government.

Dark White was supposed to be all about racial purity, but its members' motives weren't homogenous. Some originals had been true-blood believers, others thought they were betting on the favorite. And some were just

bandits.

The second-wave members, not so much older than me, those I never did sort out by motive. It didn't matter. I knew where I wanted to go, and I wouldn't be taking any of them with me.

The true-bloods were both City-and-Sector-born, an arm's length alliance that had held until the last threads unraveled. But the robberies were all City-side, and it was the City they targeted for rule.

The total take was somewhere between thirteen and fifteen million. Lucky numbers. Stashed where only the original Triangle could get at it. Not paying interest, but always drawing some. None of the Triangle ever saw a courtroom, so the money was still out there. If the location had been passed along, it would have been known to three of the second-wave leaders—true believers live to leave legacies.

I had gone under to find that stash. Not to be a hero, to be rich. Not rich to buy things, rich enough that I could jump the Membrane for the last time, live in the City forever. Live as a Full-Clear.

Life has only two outcomes: get old and die, or get dead quicker.

In my birthplace, the Sector, dead can just happen. And old is weak.

Weak unless you've got money, that is. Enough money

so you can stay out of the feeding stream. I'd been playing Sector Alchemy all my life, using iron to turn up gold. That hadn't ever worked for long, and never paid all that much.

Even so, I wouldn't have gone under just for Sector-safety ... that's never permanent. I only sat down at the Dark White table to play for a stake that would buy me all the way out.

The ink was supposed to get me close. My skills were supposed to do the rest. I was working my way through the short list of second-wave members, getting nearer to the center with every prove-in I passed. Then it all unraveled.

We knew the City Powers didn't care about putting second-wave leaders on trial any more than they had the originals. Maybe they wanted the money back, maybe they didn't give a damn. Or maybe the money was as poisoned as some said it was.

I knew this much: you start a sentence with "Maybe," and everything after that would always be true. I wasn't going to play my life on a rumor or a myth, so I went cautious. Stayed patient.

Patience still kept me short of "sure." Life's ante isn't voluntary; it comes with birth. So we all play. When we do, it's for unmarked chips. We can't know what those are worth until we turn them in.

But when it came to Dark White, we all knew how the City Powers played: Kill or capture. Capture and interrogate. Interrogate and kill.

Some members went down in gunfire. Those still alive cyber-hailed the dead as martyrs to the cause. And kept running.

Some knew the end was coming, and chose their own.

It finally got down to three men, two from the original Triangle. And me. I was a soldier, not a leader. But by then I knew there was a map. Within reach.

I was known for firearms, never moved without at least a couple holstered, maybe another in my hand. So the other two spent a lot of time disarming me before we all sat down.

Those two surviving leaders had made a lot of mistakes. Bad judgments. Fatal errors.

Thinking that taking my guns was disarming me, that was their last one.

I came Inside with most of the body art I still carry. The spider web circling my elbow, that one I earned in there.

But before the prison artist had ever switched on that homemade tattoo gun, I'd turned off all the other

switches: Anger. Sex. Hate. One I kept. Fear. Morphed it into a working paranoia that became second nature.

I'd walked in ready. Bred for the climate, trained for the conditions. Inside a ballistic-plastic cage in a world with no guns, I put more backs against the wall as I passed than the guards did. The reverb scanners they use Inside are flawless. Anything more than a couple of grams of metal is instantly detected and traced, so the only shanks are obsidian. The black glass is perfect for slicing, but useless for stabbing. Accuracy and touch is the assassin's art, a fatal flick—the carotid, the femoral—its highest form.

I was safer Inside than I'd ever been in the Sector. Even with all that ink on display, race war wasn't a pull for me. I spent more time—more of *my* time—doing work on whites than I did on nons. For those driven-insane shot-callers doing their life in Iso, the idea of calling a shot *off* never occurred.

They got me access to all the obsidian I wanted, but I didn't always need it to do my work. A liver strike is as noiseless as a blade, and popping the Adam's apple of a paralyzed man never takes long.

Halfway through my bit, I stopped taking contracts. Plenty knew what I did, but I wasn't aligned and I wasn't a player, so a contract out on me would have been stupid— the risk-reward math would never add up.

I did my days reciting the antidote to the venom that is the birthright of every Sector-born: "You can't make up for lost time ... but you can get paid for it."

Maybe I still could. Time would have passed no matter where I passed it. But time was coming hard now, closing the distance on me.

I did the math in my mind, over and over. I would either still win the stake I'd been playing for, or lose the whole race early. Either way, I'd be done working. All done.

The City is hard-line zoned: Business, Residential, Industrial, Entertainment. Fiery signage clearly marks the no-passport-required borders.

Past all those zones, on the other side of the Membrane, the Sector lurks, nesting like a dark spot on an X-ray. Viewed from a distance, you could convince yourself it was benign. But close up, all illusion vanishes.

The Sector is a cellar of poisonous mushrooms under an ever-shifting floor of perma-smog. If you want to stand under the sun, you have to find yourself another place to stand.

Between the City and the Sector is the throbbing Membrane: osmotic if you have the paper, impenetrable if

you don't. Some City-borns visit the Sector because of what they hear is on offer there. Not all of those return. Some Sector-born visit the City on a business permit. Those are easy enough to get, but they're all time-limited and cyber-tracked.

When it comes to trade, the Sector has what's wanted in the City—exotic botanicals, micro-crafted mechanicals, miniature animals, human organs. The City has laws against smuggling, but it's such a fact of life that border bribery isn't expected or demanded. The City has nothing to offer in exchange except life-supplies and precious metals, and all that traffic is legal.

The tourist business runs in both directions and the Membrane never closes. But visitors aren't allowed to stay past their permits. It's a simple rule: if you overstay and get caught, you don't get to leave.

Even virtual visitors to the Sector aren't anywhere near as safe as they seem to believe. The cyber-badger game is a thriving business: the mark thinks he's flirting with some sweet-body woman, and that he's the one moving the joystick control. Then it comes. A flirty little message: "Would you like to see a *special* picture of me?" When the mark clicks his mouse, the trap snaps. Soon, a message from someone who says the woman he's been flirting with isn't a woman at all. She's a girl. A 13-year-old girl. And by downloading that photo, he's just completed sexual

contact with a minor. That's years Inside if the badger decides to notify the City authorities.

Of course, there's an alternative.

At the back of the Sector is the river. On its far side, the launch pad to a network of roads, drivers and vehicles waiting. Some roads take you to the border. Across that border, the Pure Zone. You need a passport for the river, and a ticket for the edge of the Pure Zone.

The drivers can't enter the Pure Zone—machines don't work in there. They won't wait outside for you to return, even if pre-paid. That's what the call-words are for ... words you buy in the Sector.

From writings and rumor and myth, there are other places beyond the City, a backdoor, like the one out of the Sector to the river. But there's no way to know if those are true travelogues or wishful tales. The e-Library has all kinds of info on those supposed places, but the graffiti sprayed throughout the Sector runs about fifty-fifty on their truth. It's said that the City is the only departure point: train stations, bus depots, airports. But those are only open to City-borns, so none of us have ever left ... not as far as ever has been known.

But plenty of us have disappeared.

The Full-Clears don't talk. And we wouldn't believe them if they did.

In the Sector, no one carries papers except the tourists.

And in the City, papers won't protect you no matter how authentic they look. If you're not a true Full-Clear, paper is worthless. The police carry retinal scanners for Wants and Warrants. If you come up even Partial-Clear, those little devices will switch to camera-catch, and then you're done.

There's only two ways to come up Full-Clear off a retinal scan. One is your hologram birth certificate—all City-borns are scanned at birth. But they scan the birth-mother, too, and DNA-extract to find the bio-father, no matter what name is declared. Even though there's no way to defeat those scans, pregnant women still try and slip through the Membrane and give birth in the City. That never works—some get deported, some disappear.

The other way to be Full-Clear is to buy a new birth-scan. Eight million is the minimum, and it has to be in paper currency, checked bill-by-bill. So the actual price is closer to twelve if the currency has to be washed. Betting on Government corruption is still a gamble, but paying off for a Full-Clear isn't much of one—that tiny capillary in the financial bloodstream has always been too profitable to pinch off.

If you're not native-born, trying to live City-side comes down to your personal sensors against their constant surveillance. The City's labor camps are worse than its prisons, but you can buy your way out of either one. And

enough money will get you deep into The City, where there's places to hide.

But if you can't pass the retinal scan, all you can really buy is time.

That's the cross-Membrane connection: currency. The form varies with the location. In the Sector, paper money is unacceptable, worthless. That's because the Sector is where the finest counterfeiting is produced. Not just money, but valuables like blackmail tools. With modern equipment, anyone can fake a B&W photo, and age it so it looks like it was taken a decade ago ... but only the sharpest eye, the best equipment, and the finest hand can fake the negatives. Values vary with location. That's why no one carries ID in the Sector unless they're planning to sell it to someone else.

The Pure Zone doesn't take paper, either. There, "currency" is just code-talking for "barter."

In the City, all forms are accepted.

Flophouse-level currency will get you into the City; penthouse-level will let you stay ... until you're caught.

Caught. That's the thing, that's what you can't avoid. If you pay to hide, your money will run out. Even if it didn't, so what? If you can't move freely within the City, take what it has to offer, you might as well never have left the Sector.

For someone with my destination, there was only the

one path.

The alley welcomed me as if I'd never been away. Enveloped me, more like, darkness thickening as I walked its length. The deepest black wasn't just a color shift; it carried the weight and substance of squid ink.

The Sector is anarchy. Not the "anarchy" they whisper about in the City, not even what the e-Library says about it. The Sector may have some wild people, but nobody can run amok for long. There's no mayor, no city council, no police ... but there are rules. And enforcement.

Just like the City, the Sector has industries. And pirates. Just like the City, when people rush toward a body lying in an alley their goals range from rescue to salvage.

There's no hospitals in the Sector. There's healers, potion-brewers, craftspeople ... even emergency centers for body damage. But no hospitals, no operating facilities. If a Sector-child needs a bone marrow transplant, or radio-chemo or anything like that, that has to be done City-side, so the script is written differently. If the parents don't have currency, that's when the Sector's collectors make the rounds. Different collectors visit different places. And ask different ways. But the answer is always the same. That's the rules—you don't kick in, your name

gets known. Once that happens, no one knows you.

In the City, government provides everything: fuel, power, water, sewage ... all the way down to the supposedly forbidden. It's all for sale, and those who can pay the most get the best of what there is. There are elections, but the candidates are all fungible goods—the "choices" are nothing but palatable illusions.

In the Sector, anarchy rules. So the people have become a survival-driven organism, self-regulating to accommodate everything from temperature to threat. Nothing is wasted; nothing goes to waste.

Some say anarchy first began in the City, maybe fifty years ago. It was a threat to the Powers, so it had to be extinguished. But the Powers finally learned from their own past. They understood that you can't kill anarchy ... you can only kill anarchists. So they killed all they could find, and drove the rest down a narrow chute toward the Membrane.

They did that because the City powers know how things work. How every living thing works. What you don't kill grows, so their task is to control the size of the container.

You can even let the dimensions of that container flex ... so long as you have the power to keep it sealed.

That's safer than trying to pull anarchy out by its root. Because even if you chop that root down to tiny pieces,

even if you grind the pieces into powder and scatter them across stone, new growth is always possible. Always to be feared.

Immune to change, these alleys. Packing crates stacked like the e-Library pictures of Hong Kong slums. Privacy always dearly-bought. At the very top, sawtooth roofs strain to catch smog-filtered light from a never-seen sun. At the bottom, all light is artificial. At all levels, violence is very real.

I moved past an old man seated on a cut-down oil drum. "I mark you," he quavered in a cancer-chemo voice, acknowledging his own forthcoming death with neither surprise nor terror.

Not fearless, indifferent.

Not the "don't mind dying" song of the anchored Sector gangster and his traveling forefather, the bluesman.

Not the maudlin "I've had a good life."

Just no reason to believe that whatever's coming next is going to be any better than what already is.

I'd been that kind of indifferent to life ever since I could remember. Not courageous, just infused with a dull lack of concern for whatever might show up. Death, just another door to the same room. As a young man, I'd

courted that feeling. Older now, I know it for what it truly is: a crippling handicap.

That's why I kept fear with me when I entered prison. Treasured it, even. Without fear, the warning signals are blocked ... and intellect alone has never been sufficient to protect any of our species. So I took every corner wide, felt every vibration across my back, operated on auto-scan.

In the Sector, I still take those corners. Still enter those places.

Because I'm still watching for a way out.

The bottle tree grew without sunlight. It stood disdainfully aloof between a pair of louvered metal crates that the ganja dealers rent to buyers who wanted to hot-box their purchases. I tapped its glass leaves with a silver coin, playing the doorbell tune. Blue, red, clear, blue.

The alley went quiet.

I took out a gold piece—a demi-Tiger, easily worth a grand even on a snap-sale, depending on the day's quote. The orange glass descended. I dropped in the coin. They'd have an assay-app scanner with a color range on the other end: set to Reject at 10K, Caution-Accept at 14, Plus-graded all the way to 24, bar-coded.

A yellow glass dropped down. Offering accepted. I

added two more.

Three is the sacred number. Universal, across all lines.

The air displaced behind me. I didn't turn around.

"Who do you hate?" the voice said.

"I have no hate," I answered.

"Because you have forgiven?"

"Because I'm empty," I answered again, echoing the clue from the old man at the alley's mouth.

"Go to the goat," the voice said.

I worked my codex. The goat without horns? A child, then? A child to be sacrificed?

No. I hadn't been a child since I could remember. And no child could answer my questions, or point the way for me.

So, Azazel? The scapegoat? But that was Hebrew, and the Michael I had consulted was riding a cross. So it would be a Judas goat I was meant to find.

Not *my* Judas. Him I'd found halfway through my sentence, when they brought him in on new charges. So...? Someone knew the killer I was looking for? If that was the message, how was it supposed to help me?

It took a while to cycle through, but then it locked. A Judas always has a price. The gelt had to be out there, first.

The ground had to be seeded.

That I knew how to do.

This deep in, impossible to tell time of day—shadow is 24/7. In the Sector, cops are limited to perimeter routes; they can't go deep. They're not there to protect the natives, and tourists with enough weight bring their own protectors.

The perimeter is where they put the labor crews. I watched the prisoners. Each man moved at a choreographed tai chi pace, barely displacing the molecules of air around him, profoundly disinterested in the frantic activity only a short distance from their task.

My eyes shifted to where guards had the man who had tried to run surrounded, electric prods readied.

While they were still threatening the runner with what was next on their menu, he was already dining off his own. Chomping down on the capsule that would take him over any wall.

I didn't have any fresh trust built up, and I didn't want to use up old IOUs on hardware. So I tried a few stalls, always asking for Igor. It didn't take long. A Frankenstein

is a pistol built from no-serial-number parts, the barrel one-time turned, the grip a wrap of rubber bands over swirled plastic. They have O-ringed suppressor stacks, only take sub-sonic loads. In a village of air guns and crossbows, gunfire noise would be fatal to the shooter, like dipping yourself in radium before going hunting in the dark.

A Frankenstein is untraceable if you follow the rule.

Just the one: Don't use it twice.

I bought two of them, from different stalls.

The Sector doesn't resemble the City. It has no signposts, no numbers on its unnamed streets, no windows advertising the goods carried in the shops. The street-level joints have no windows at all. The maps sold to tourists are as trustworthy as a playground candyman. Hiring a guide was all word-of-mouth, some of that from the mouths of liars.

But the graffiti hadn't changed in the years I'd been away, and I found the first sprayed message easy enough:

Two bookended "F"

words meant two corners down, four words total meant four flights up.

Such messages are never over-tagged, the unseen "Protected By" keeps them untouched.

The man who paid the Tagger was sitting behind his drafting table in a room with no door.

I'd doubted he could help—even the finest cryptographer can't crack Psychotic—but he was worth the little it cost to try.

I knew some of the language: obsession is power, relentlessness trumps resistance. But each member of that tribe has his own music. Their messages meant not only whatever they meant, they meant it only *when* they did.

So I told the man what I knew, and he told me what he knew. Together, it added up to a meal that wouldn't endanger even a morbidly obese diabetic with advanced aortic blockage.

Back to the street, back to reading the signs. Some were directions, some were just clues to puzzles I'd learned to solve before I was old enough to steal on my own.

Like seeing a man using a pay phone. In August. Wearing gloves.

The tag I was looking for wouldn't be on any particular

wall. I didn't want a territory marker, I wanted a "work in progress" statement.

If you were a City-born businessman, that meant "blind copy," a notation telling the recipient he was the other half of a twosome that left the third party in the dark. If he trusted the sender, that is.

But under the Sector's canopy, "bcc:" was the tag of the Building Climbers Crew. Their trademark was high-altitude Parkour—a crew of flying thieves who soared between shadows and never took more than one fall.

I stood where they could see me. Lit a cigarette to show I was prepared to wait. Kept my hands in sight.

Time passed. Shadow-breakers buzzed my vision like darting sparrows. Then one of them dropped to the ground, landing as lightly as a venomous butterfly.

He was thin. Rope-muscled, with blue-blazed hair. Gloves and sneakers designed for his work. No elbow pads or knee guards—the bcc: always worked without a net.

"You want what?" he said, his voice years older than his body.

"I want E.J.," I told him. "I know he's gone. At the time he left, I couldn't come to pay my respects. Now, I can. And that's what I mean to do."

"You knew E.J.?"

"He was my friend."

"Say his name."

"Ed Jerr."

"Edger."

"He was. And, the way it came to me, that's how he left."

"What came to you was true. You know the limit-words, then?"

"You try for the sky, you're willing to die."

"You know what to say. But I don't know you. And I *did* know Edger. I knew *all* the crew who went before I took my place. So...?"

"So this: if you think I came here looking for information, information that you'd have, you'd be right. I don't expect you to trust a stranger, so I won't insult you with money. And I won't embarrass myself by trying to use force. But I came for two reasons: the one you think—the info, yes; and one of my own—the one I said. You only get to say on the first one. You don't have to tell me anything you don't want to. But I'm here to pay my respect to Edger, and that you won't stop me from doing."

He watched me, not moving. Dark forms closed in.

I took a small black bottle from my jacket pocket. Razor Cognac, Edger's score-celebration drink. I dropped to one knee, and spoke:

"I don't know the spot where you fell, brother. So I mark this spot as yours, now."

I poured an "X" onto the concrete.

"See you soon enough," I said. And got to my feet.

I was almost to the corner when a voice came: "Wait."

When I turned, there were three of them.

The first one who'd dropped spoke. "If you're who you say, if you're who you say you were to Edger, you know the Recording Wall."

"I don't know it," I told him, code-talking as I felt more shadows fill the untrustworthy light. "No outsider can know it, and I was never a member. But I know where it is. Would that tell you enough?"

"Enough to test. Will you climb with us?"

"You know I can't do that."

"Why can you not? If you knew Edger...."

"I already said I was never a member," I told him. Then I switched to no-code truth: "I had the strength," I said, speaking with the quiet gravity required for honor-talk. "I had the speed. I even had the balance. But I didn't have

the depth. Up close, I could do everything Edger could do. Better, in fact. And that's what I did."

A sharp intake of breath from one of the other two flanking their chief was the only response.

"You put in work?" the one with blue-blazed hair asked.

"Another test?" I answered his question with my own. "I know the bcc: doesn't contract. I know you handle your own business in the Sector. But Edger had to cross the Membrane a number of times. If you knew him, you knew why. You know the rule."

"Tell us," he said.

"Some practice to better know, some risk to become better known."

"And for those who learn? For those who become better?"

"Everybody climbs by themselves ... but nobody climbs alone," I recited their creed.

"The one that went across with Edger those times, that was you?"

"It was," I said.

"Where were you born?"

"In the night."

"Not when, where?

"I just said."

"Say your name, then."

"Carbon."

"That's a dangerous name to claim."

"For anyone else, it could be," I said, adding a slight bow to soften my words.

"All we've heard.... But you never joined?"

"It's my eyes," I told them. "I can't measure distances. I don't mean I'm far-sighted or near-sighted or anything like that. I don't need glasses. I can hold a ledge with my fingers, I can walk on my hands, I can drop from heights. But I can't judge how far to fly. Too deep, too short ... never just right."

"You can learn to—"

"—I tried," I interrupted. "All I learned was how to fall. Edger could work blindfolded. He could feel distances I couldn't even *see*. I could do some things, yes. But I'd always be ... limited."

"And you couldn't take that? You still could have joined. Still have been a full—"

"I couldn't take that," I admitted, in the voice of the deeply disaffected man-child I had once been. "There's only three ways out of the Sector. The City ... plenty go, few stay. Stay alive, anyway. The Pure Zone ... who knows? The third path, Edger's path, that was the sky. We came up together. If I couldn't ride right next to him, I didn't want to ride at all."

The three of them stepped back. That's when I saw one

of them was a girl. She wasn't hiding it, just not putting it out there.

I watched them talk, their faces turned sideways in case I could read lips.

They came back toward me.

"You won't know how to find the building, and it's not marked. But you'll know the floor."

"Thirteen," I said.

"Follow us," the girl answered, as if completing a riddle.

We walked for maybe twenty minutes. No one barred our way, but everyone watched. We stopped in front of a jagged tower I didn't recognize.

"This is it," the chief said. "You say you can't climb as we do. All right—we'll climb your way. With you."

The place was an active hive, but no one moved toward us until the tenth floor. The man who stepped forward was a bullethead, about double my weight. "He does barriers," a kid sitting on a wooden crate said. "Place for stop, lift for pay."

Before I could ask the toll price, the humongo grabbed a thick rectangular pillar of what looked like ferrite that was standing against the wall. He hoisted it to his shoulder

with a professional lifter's grunted exhale, and carried it to where the four of us stood. He dropped to one knee and laid the pillar before us like he was unrolling a rug. He stepped back, mammoth arms too muscle-bowed to touch his sides.

"Just a trick," I said.

"A trick?" the kid's voice sneered. "Then *you* lift it."

"Your man didn't lift it," I answered. "Not from the ground. It was standing, leaning against the wall. He just shifted it to his shoulder from there. But there's no way to grip it lying flat as it is now."

"Then how did it get to where he took it from?"

"I don't know," I shrugged. "Maybe took a dozen of you, working with levers. Or maybe a block-and-tackle. Hydraulics, air pumps ... there's lots of ways. But you've got some system going. One you use all the time."

"That's just a guess."

"Here's another, then. I'm guessing your man can't put it back where he got it from. Not alone."

"So you won't pay the toll?"

"I didn't say that," I said.

"Two gold," the borderlord said.

"One," I replied, knowing what was expected.

The thirteenth floor was empty except for stacks of concrete squares. They looked precisely uniform, no distinguishing marks.

The girl pointed at a stack in a far corner. "Say your name again."

"Carbon," I spoke as if to Edger.

"Twenty-nine down," she said.

The crew member who hadn't spoken walked to a stack and began removing the squares from the top down, handling them as easily as if they were plastic poker chips. When he got down to where he wanted, he pulled a square free and carried it over to us. In one hand.

At a gesture from the girl, he turned over the square, revealing the handprint I'd placed in the wet concrete so many years ago. At another gesture from the girl, I walked to the opposite corner.

She dropped to her knees and mixed a little batch of concrete, then poured it into a wood frame. She held up one hand in a "Wait!" gesture.

A few minutes later: "Now."

I knelt and placed my left hand down into the wet concrete, holding carefully to keep the impression as clear as I knew the other one would be.

Then we waited.

I put a pack of cigarettes on another stack. The girl took one. I lit it for her. Then I lit my own.

"You're sure, aren't you?" their chief said.

"Cradle to grave," I told him. Words to convey commitment, not coverage. I didn't remember my cradle, and Edger had out-raced me to the grave. But we'd come up together, climbing the milestones.

"They're the same," the girl told the other two.

"Put the new one back," the chief told the silent one.

When he returned, the chief handed the original to me.

"A gift from Edger," he said.

I handed the slab to the silent one, a hawk-faced youth with a long black ponytail. He knew what to do, holding it in two hands facing me. My first strike cracked the concrete. I snapped the individual pieces into smaller ones, working until there was nothing but dust. I used my hands to cup some of the dust into a tiny pile, then I swept the pile into a little leather bag and handed it to the chief.

"I know I can't visit a departure place," I said, formally. "I would be honored if you would add this to my friend's last path." I was speaking of a vapor trail, not a grave. There are no ground-burials in the Sector, only

crematoriums ... some run as a business, some homemade. If the bcc: accepted my request, the dust from my mark—my *true* mark, not some added-on skin ink—would be tossed from the same spot where they'd said goodbye to Edger.

Each time the bcc: visited that spot, they'd get across on a wood bridge dropped between buildings. Each time they left, they'd burn that bridge.

He bowed his head, brought his fists together, then interlaced his fingers and touched the first knuckle of his right hand to his forehead.

I returned the gesture on pure muscle-memory.

When we descended to the tenth floor, the ferrite pillar was still lying across the corridor. The silent one pointed at it, looked a question at me. I nodded.

Together, we braced our feet against the wall, put our palms on the top of the pillar and walked it upright, as if we'd spent years rehearsing the move. When it stood against the far wall, I crouched and tipped it back toward me, taking it on my shoulder. Then I walked it past the kid on the wooden crate, all the way over to where the humongo had taken it from ... and tipped it against the wall.

The kid on the wooden crate held out the gold piece.

I shook my head in refusal. "You know who my friends are. You know they don't need to climb stairs to reach your floor. Any floor. But, me, I needed your stairs. So your toll was fair."

"We don't charge tolls for friends."

"Say more."

"We want to be friends," the kid said, holding out the gold piece again. That time, I took it.

Sector daylight is oyster shell, gray dominating white. Here, the weather is the climate. The air is odor-imprisoning thick. Almost visible.

Daylight itself has no meaning. I learned that as a child. Darkness always threatens to encroach. Feeling that, the darkness inside me would rise in response. A doomed battle, with an outcome more certain than any forecast.

Walking alone, I saw the next message:

"The Sights" was Sector-speak for 2020, the last year the City Powers had attempted to enforce their own laws

on this side of the Membrane. Now, they just patrol the perimeter.

Risking it all to leave this place, to *stay* another place, that's what sent me to prison.

Now I'm back. Returning for another exit key.

The flickering arrows told me I was close.

After a few twists and turns and one full double-back, the arrows stopped flickering. I was in the Light District, so-called because it carried its own illumination. Not artificial, atmospheric. The alley offered a single stairway; the stairway offered a choice of tunnels. I chose the one I remembered.

I passed by the white soft-strobe above a door set flat against the tunnel wall. The lights wheeled through a spectrum as I walked: yellow, pink, amber, turquoise, lilac, lavender. Each a different choice, provided you could read the menu. As I approached the blue light, I slipped on the infra-glasses. The tunnel's door had no bulb above it, but the infra lenses picked up the red glow outlining the jamb.

Last stop, then.

On the far edge of the Sector is a river, the dumpsite for all the waste the Sector produces. Over many years, a species of electric eel evolved to occupy its depths. What they feed on nobody knows, but they have thrived. Once, there was lively betting on those who tried to swim to the other side and back. Now, nobody tries.

The river's bank is even more dangerous than its depths. You need a passport to cross on the ferry, but unless you know who to show it to, you'll never get close enough to board.

Inside the Sector, the buildings crowd each other, the sky invisible from the ground, no matter where you stand. The only passage through this favela is a venous system of Ginza-signed alleys and tunnels. Each step is a risk—shaky architecture, shakier inhabitants. Every piece of railing was gripped by some form of satellite dish, creating a self-maintaining network.

The connected cones don't block GPS signals, they spin them: an endless aikido loop that never exits, the signals moving at varying speed, but never colliding. Because it never takes root, it's unhackable. The only tracking mechanisms are human, and they're as reliable as caprice itself.

Here, greenery is the most visible symbol of wealth, tiny patches planted on protected terraces. By weight, live

sod is more costly than gold, kept alive by a latticework of sun-substitute LEDs, with nutrients pumped in by hand. Hybrid cactus is the most popular decorative—when soil replaces sand, it's usually for cultivating poisons. Belladonna, wolfsbane, rosary peas ... anything that can be tinctured down or intensified up, depending on the result sought. And the price per gram.

Because there's no sun, Sector-dwellers have perfected indoor grow-lighting way beyond anything you can find in the City. That's why it's worth moving Sector marijuana across the Membrane—it brings twenty times the price of City-grown weed. That's one of the draws for tourists, too, the vapo-lounges.

No point trying to stop a protractor at some point in its ceaseless circles, so I went right to its spike-planted foot to pick up the keys. No argument from him—the rent had been paid every month for twenty years, before and after prison, uninterrupted. I knew the payments would be kept up as long as I was alive—most of the money I'd left behind had been on the streets, throwing off interest. Even with the occasional cost of collection, it was a perpetual motion small-money machine.

Some use prison time to learn. Pretty much everyone

reads, but that's not the same as learning. There's plenty of porn, published outside and smuggled in. Written inside, too. Sometimes sold, sometimes traded, usually juggled ... loaned out at shark rates. But the most popular books are mysteries. Those are the same as the porn: a few rotating plots, the same sort of characters, filled with filler— descriptions of restaurants, clothing, buildings, brand-names. The hero is usually some ex-cop who had to leave the force because he was a drunk. Or shot someone by accident. Or took a stand against corruption. When he's facing a showdown, he goes down to his basement and pumps iron. Or hits the heavy bag. There's always at least one woman. Always sex, always well-performed. All the same. Circular slop, failed escapes. No taste in any of those meals, just enough nourishment to let you take the next bite, like those Nutri-loaf slabs they shove through the door slots in Iso.

I used my key to enter the apartment the bcc: had already safety-scanned. As I stepped inside, a young woman slid off a salvaged couch and reached toward her purse. I showed her the Frankenstein as I hissed a harsh *sssssss!* She froze. I flashed my fingers: three, zero, three. She turned and stepped into the bedroom. Came out with a tall man about her age. They each picked up one of the carry-ons that had been standing next to the door. She

dropped two keys on the rag-rug as they walked out, closing the door behind them, leaving the TV on.

It took me less than an hour to satisfy myself that no one had entered any of the closets, exposed or hidden.

At a guarded stall, I pulled a silk square off the slate tray. A color wheel, with a black center. I twisted it to scarlet and tucked it into the breast pocket of the midnight blue shantung suit I'd taken from the apartment's closet. The suit had been waiting for me, its custom-cut jacket with the nylon mesh inside pockets tailored to fit whatever I needed to carry.

Three stalls down, I bought a little bag of glass balls. Five colors, five surface finishes. I might have to work in total darkness, and it wouldn't do to drop death where I meant to drop deception.

Next, three Sector-limited mobile phones, all unused.

Rasp hadn't heard my voice for some time, but that didn't matter. His number never changes. And I'd made sure he knew I was still around, tapping him from bootleg cells that cost dearly in prison and couldn't be used more

than a couple of times, max. Getting rid of them was harder than getting them in—the guards double the price for exits, and the money can't come off your commissary books.

He answered like he always does, just his own brand of sandpaper growl, to let me know the channel was open. Rasp didn't get his name from his voice. A rasp is a harsh file, and he'd been very good with one.

"I'm hunting," I told him.

» » »

"No name. No description. Just a pattern."

» » »

Then I told him what I had.

He was offline for a few minutes. The hum didn't change, so I left the connection open.

"The guy you want is Sonar," he harshed out.

"Sonar?" I said, to make certain I'd gotten the pronunciation right.

"Yesss...." he gave it a couple of beats, then: "Sonar. He hears everything."

In the Sector, there's no such thing as privacy, only little nodules of dead air. Hovering, quiet as a crop duster's clouds. Sonar wouldn't be easy to run down—

anyone looking for him wouldn't ever be the only one.

There's no privacy in prison, either. A murky aquarium with no shortage of sharks. Plenty of remora, too, but no danger from any of their kind. In that ocean, only the moray eels are feared.

I'd studied, and I'd learned. Metaphysics and kinetics, book and body. Then the test beds: humans. To survive, to keep proving-in, to earn. To stay honed.

So when I found Sonar, I traded for what he wanted most. Not gold, a secret far more valuable: I told him how I'd found him.

Not the truth, of course. But a good enough story to ensure that he'd contact Rasp when he found a new spot to listen from.

The Sector is a place where all important words are always left unsaid, like those blacked-out parts in the government documents some defense lawyers file motions to get. Some of the graffiti lasts as long as a finger snap, as valued as a whore's promise. But some is permanent. And posted everywhere:

a secret told
is a soul sold

I found what I was looking for in one of the lizard-breeding shops. The tiny hamster running on the treadmill wasn't being patient, he was going over the same ground endlessly, like the GPS signals that never stop bouncing around the Sector. I watched the scene for a while, studying close. I saw it clear—I could work the Sector forever, but I'd never find the map I needed.

But that wasn't the real lesson. This was: the hamster wheel was a technique ... like one of the combat forms I'd studied so deeply. You don't engage your enemy, you turn him. Not his body, his force. Re-direct that force. *Spin* it. Disrupt his balance until he exhausts himself by firing his never-connect strikes.

The longer you keep the enemy turning, the closer you are. To him, and to ending it.

I saw it.

Clear.

Now.

All my searching was being turned, doomed to fail. So I jumped off the wheel.

My first stop was the one bank where I'll always have an account. I don't like all my memories, but I do trust them.

I was a very young man when I'd found the spot for the first time. Carefully following the instructions I'd earned guarding a goods-for-gold transfer point, I tapped the number into the keypad a narrow spotlight had illuminated.

There's probably other words for what I was, then. To say my age, I mean. In the Sector, if you're proven old enough to do certain things, then that's your age. I'd done a man's work guarding the goods, snapped a robber's arm and killed his partner—the one with the Frankenstein. So it didn't matter how many years I had on my calendar. I didn't even know where that calendar would be. Didn't matter, not on the Sector's growth chart— I had killed a man for pay, so I was a man.

"Now, now, now, now.... *Now!*" the busty redhead

whisper-screamed, scarlet nails clawing the back of my neck and the base of my spine as she bucked underneath me.

It wasn't like I'd imagined it would be, but I followed her down to the end.

"Give me one," she said, as soon as my cigarettes came out.

I did. She pushed against me until I understood what she wanted, and rolled onto my back.

"It's good luck, you know," she said.

"What is?"

"First-timers. It's good luck for a girl to get one. You didn't ask for me. It was just my turn. That was luck, too. I'll play a number tomorrow. One, one two."

"Next time, I'll ask for you," I told her.

"Yeah? How would you do that? What's my name?"

"I don't need your name. I could ... I could describe you. To the man at the door."

"Plu? That slob? He doesn't make the call-outs. The Charge Lady does that. All Plu does is stand around and look tough. Did he scare you?"

"No."

"Just ... "No," huh? How old are you, anyway?"

"I don't know. Not for sure. What does it matter?"

"Does it matter to you how old I am?

"No. No, it doesn't."

"Cherry. That's my name. Cherry."

"Cherry."

"Cherry. You know what that means?"

"It's a red—"

"—It means a girl's flower. A cherry—the kind *you* meant—that's a fruit. A very sweet fruit, if you know how to handle it. But it starts out as a blossom. Kind of a shield over a girl's pussy. Once that's taken, it's gone forever. You understand? You're only a virgin once."

"What difference?"

She propped herself on her elbow, looked down at me.

"You actually mean that?"

"I don't know what you're asking. Anything you do for the first time, every single thing you do for the first time, you can't do for the first time *again*, sure. But you can do it over and over, right? So I can't see what difference it makes."

"This was your first time," she whispered. Not a question.

"And I could do it again," I said. Not an answer.

"You could. And you could do it better, too."

"I don't see how it could be better."

"Ah, you're a silver-tongue."

"A ... what?"

"A sweet-talker."

"I don't think so. Nobody ever said that about me."

"You never did this before," she said. "And if—"

A hard palm-slap on the door to her little thin-walled room.

"Time's up!" a man's voice came through the panel.

"Round two!" the girl called out, no sweetness in her voice. She turned to me, said, "Plu, he actually frightens some of the ... clients."

"And they get dressed and leave?"

"Some do. Some pay for another go. Like you're going to."

"There's other things we could do," Cherry told me, the next week. "You could do them to me; I could do them to you, too."

"Not the same—"

"Not exactly the same things, no—we're not constructed that way. Here's how it's going to go. You do what you want, first."

"Right now."

"Yes, right now. And then, round two, I'll do what *I* want. Is that fair?"

"It seems like it is."

"Even though you're the one paying?"

"Paying to learn is fair."

"A silver-tongue, for true," she whispered.

"You know what this is?" she asked me, holding a fat squeeze-tube in her hand.

"Some kind of—"

"—It's a lubricant. Women are supposed to get wet. Down there. Get wet when they're excited. It's what the clients expect. Like moaning. Or using my nails."

"Do you need—"

"That's up to you," she whispered. "Do you want to be a client? Or do you want to be a man?"

"This could be the hardest part," she said, the week after.

"What else could there—"

"You did what you wanted, yes?"

"Yes."

"And then I did what I wanted?"

"If you say so."

"I say so. Now it gets to another part. You say what you

want me to do. And I'll do it."

"And then?"

"In round two?"

"Yes."

"In round two, you do what *I* want you to do."

"I don't promise."

"Why not?"

"Because I don't know what you're going to want. And I don't break promises."

"You don't break promises? Everybody breaks—"

"—I don't. That's what I'm known for. If I say I'm going to do something—"

"—How could you be 'known' for anything? You can't be more than—"

"—I am, though. Known, I mean. I don't break promises. That's all I have. That's my currency."

"So…. You know my name. What's yours, then?"

"Carbon."

"Carbon? What kind of name is that?"

"A man gave it to me. A man I met. In a place. A place where we talked a lot. There wasn't anything else to do, and we had to stay there for a while. That man, he knew a lot. About a lot of things. He said that carbon is an element. Like copper. Or gold."

"Gold is—"

"—That's what I thought, when he first told me. Why couldn't I be gold? Carbon, that's just some black rock. But what he said was that carbon is a special element. You put it under enough pressure, if it doesn't ... get crushed, you know what it turns into?"

"What?"

"A diamond," I said, maybe proud to be telling her something she didn't know. "The hardest thing there is."

"A precious stone. All the girls want those."

"Diamonds?"

"Precious stones. There's all kinds. Even diamonds, there's all kinds. All colors, too. The most valuable, they've got no color. Those're called 'flawless.'"

"No one's ever going to call me that."

"You don't want to do that?" Cherry asked me.

"I don't think so. It doesn't sound—"

"—If you do it, if you learn how to do it *good*, every woman's going to love you."

"No, they won't."

"How could you know?"

"Because ... because it doesn't add up right. People love what you do, it doesn't mean they love *you.*"

"That old man tell you that, too?"

"Nobody had to tell me that."

She was quiet all through round two. Then: "Are you coming back?"

"Yes," I told her.

"A promise?"

I told her, "Yes." Again.

"The world's black and white," Cherry said. "Black and white."

"There's other colors. Like you said about diamonds, right? Even your name—"

"No colors that count," she said, very softly. "Black and white, there's colors *between* those two. But those aren't real colors, just reflections."

"I don't think that's right," I told her, although I suddenly wasn't so sure.

"You'll see. If there had to be a color exactly between black and white, you know what it would be?"

"No."

"Blue. That's the color of life."

"I don't understand what you're saying."

"My life," she said. "Your life, too."

It wasn't until another lifetime that I did more thinking about what Cherry had told me then. Prison is good for thinking. Solitary thinking works best in solitary. My name. Carbon. Pressure doesn't always form diamonds. Inside, some take pills to escape. Or drink the home-brew. Those are temporary. Some hang up and go away permanent. But some feel that same pressure like pus inside a wound. And know the way to expel that pus is to apply pressure on themselves. Healing through pain.

I chose that.

The time between my visits got longer and longer. Cherry always asked me that same question. I always gave her the same answer. I guess, in my mind, it was a permanent thing between us.

But when I came back there after I got out, Cherry was gone. I asked the man at the door—Plu was gone, too—where I could find her. He didn't know. I asked the lady in charge. She told me she didn't know either.

But she knew the answer to the question I'd come there to ask.

Every visible centimeter of her was symmetrically synthetic: implant-augmented, free-standing breasts; perfectly pulped lips that had never felt a bee's sting; reshaped nose; ears pinned and de-lobed; eyelashes so long they threw shadows over her cheekbones. Even her aureoles were infused with pink, as if any deviation from Blonde was taboo. Perfect dimples had been inserted just above her impossibly rounded bottom, a beauty mark added to one cheek to break the symmetry, creating an illusion of authenticity. Her legs were just short of muscular, with prominent flex-lines on the outside of her thighs, each calf clearly defined. Full-body derma-abrasion kept the seamless hypoallergenic coating in a state of barely-human, no-pores perfection. More investments had been made beneath that skin: a rib removed on each side to wasp her waist, an extra arch force-molded into her feet, titanium knees to handle the shock of five-inch heels. Her equipment included a full spectrum of contact lenses, hair weaves, interchangeable nails, chemical perfumes. Even the zipper down the back of her skirt had twin rows of little arrows pointing in opposite directions to emphasize the enhanced twitch when she turned her back to walk to the other side of her reception chamber.

But this one was no owner-created toy. No pimp had financed her transformation. Every golden drop of the

investments was hers alone, and her fake was as real as it gets. Even her heart was a transplant—it came from the factory with its own refrigerant.

A counter-puncher to her core, she watched my veiled eyes with her empty ones, ready to react. Clamp her labia or razor my throat, it was all the same to her.

In the Sector, there wasn't much she didn't know. And nothing she couldn't touch.

One thing she didn't know was me. But if she was surprised at what I wanted, her unlined face didn't show it.

She sat at the center of a web, threads carrying messages in both directions. But only line-tugs touched her core—she was a purpose-built machine.

Her voice was filtered through a reworked larynx, complete with channel selection depending on customer preference. But I wasn't a customer, so I got the metallic version.

"They have my child." the Synthetic Woman said, after she heard what I wanted from her. "Far outside, on the other side of the river and across the border. Somewhere in the Pure Zone. My network doesn't reach there. If you promise to bring her to me, I will get you any information

that exists."

She didn't have to add "in the Sector," to her promise—within it, her reach was both total and limited. I gave her words a couple of beats before I spoke.

"For my promise?" I asked. If this one had a child, she must have given birth before she'd had all that work done.

"Don't be silly," she mock-lisped. Her teeth were as perfect as her smile.

And equally unnatural.

"Do you know where to find the Transport Web?" I tried again.

"That's information," she said. It must have been an effort to sneer against the heaviness of her lips, but she managed.

"I know it is. And you already said what you want. On the other side of the river, there's only the one way over the next border into the Pure Zone ... but that information's not worth anything to me unless I go."

"Yes?" she said, very gently. Then she took a deep breath she didn't need, and waited for my response.

I paused, processing. There could be no bargaining with this one. No day-rate, no advance. Any contract would be strictly POD. But if she paid, she'd pay in full. She'd either give me the map, or have me killed.

So, a gamble. I'd come alone, but she couldn't be sure I

was alone. After all, I'd found her. And went through a couple of her shields to do that. And no matter her power, she still had to live in the Sector.

"Yes," I finally answered. "So, if I go, I go for you. Only for you. A contract. How to get to the next border, that's information, sure. But that doesn't go on my tab, and I'm not paying for it, agreed? Same for the tolls. And the supplies I'll need."

I'd been careful to say, *"If I go."* My last choice. First, I had to exhaust every other chance.

The wash from the sodium lights revealed the undercoat of bruising that radiated past the randomly spattered blood on the stuccoed wall. I followed the arrows down the tunnel.

The shaman was badly named. He looked the part— long hair the color of cigar ash, a robe adorned with purchased amulets. But he was no source of ancient wisdom, only a contact to a connection. I couldn't fill my duffel with what I'd exchanged for more of my gold, but at least there had been no bargaining—info-traders always come flat-fee.

"I don't have any to sell," said the man I'd been sent to, "but I can tell you who does."

So I paid him what he asked, too.

"I can't teach you kinetics," the next one said.

"No one can," I assured him, feigning regret.

As he transferred the gold to his robes, I showed him kinetics.

"Why do you carry the strap over different shoulders every time I see you?" the next liar asked. Recognizing my face, not my purpose.

"For balance," I told him.

"Why not carry half the weight over each shoulder, then?"

"Access," I explained, reaching into my duffel.

After that, I kept moving. Looking. Using my patience.

The woman's face was a skull, lightly coated with paper skin that would no longer hold ink. "This," she said, holding out a curved piece of steel the length of my finger, "is a tool. An object, so it has no life. What has no life has no nature. This cuts, yes. But *what* it cuts becomes its

truth. And the one who holds it decides that truth."

I was quicker with my hands than she was with her charlatan's tongue.

Yeah, it would *be the seventh one,* I thought to myself. *The Sector doesn't get sunlight, but Holy Cliché still penetrates.*

"I've got no more gold," I told him.

"I know," he said, proving himself another fraud.

"A contract, then?" I offered.

"A contract, yes. A contract *not* to act."

"Not to...."

"Not to act *this* time. You know. And now you see that I do as well."

"Yes," I agreed. "Done, then."

In the Sector, killing a shaman who false-sells isn't a crime.

"Occultism cannot travel," said the shaman whose life I'd spared, sipping a drink he hadn't offered to share.

"I don't understand."

"Can you see this?"

"That board? Sure."

"Look more closely. There are two troughs. You see the difference?"

"One's just paper. The other has some kind of ... mud, maybe? ... in it."

"Touch each."

I did. "This one, it's sandpaper. The other, it's ... sticky," I said, pulling my fingers away. It took some effort.

"Sandpaper in that one, yes. The one you last touched, quicksand. But a very thin layer, so you were able to extract yourself."

"A lesson board?"

"For those who heed, it is. Most men ... most women, too ... they will tentatively approach such choices. Touching lightly. When one feels harsh and difficult, they will choose the alternative. The one that feels cool and soothing."

"And get trapped."

"Yes. The sand *paper* is a hard road. No one walks it without pain. The quick *sand* is gentle and welcoming. But once its true nature is discovered, resistance only increases its power."

"Why show me, then? I'm not a student."

"Not of mine, no. I show you what you already know.

A choice you have already made. I show you because I already gave you everything you asked for.

"And here is more. No matter what you have been told, all magick is natural. It comes from living things, things you see and touch every day. But it is above the natural, on a different plane. What most see as magick is a summoning from that plane. That, you could be taught."

"I don't have time for lessons," I told him.

"I see you do not. Yet, you will heed this: magick is always the summoning of the spider. A tap on any strand calls it forth. It comes to kill, but, in coming, can *be* killed. So remember this, then: the mystic will always triumph over the scholar. The scholar can study the mystic, but only the mystic can *evoke.* And, for these truths, I expect you to honor your bargain with me."

"I already have," I told him.

He nodded his understanding.

The shaman pointed with a missing-tip finger, "Everything in your duffel, now has no power here." More a wish than a warning. By then, word had traveled, and they all knew what I could do without tools. Just to reach him, I'd survived a number of death warrants. But they'd all been written with glass quills tapping against my stone.

I don't make choices for others, and I don't make rules. But I do make promises, and I always keep them. One is: I swear not to care about your life any more than you care about mine.

"Where, then, does what's in my bag have power?" I asked him.

"Your destination."

"That's fair," I said. Not conceding he knew which direction I'd move in, but admitting I was going outside the Sector.

"It is. Remember the other part of our bargain—whatever you do not use, you must return."

"That's fair, too," I said, playing along with his face-saving lie.

When I left that last one's tunnel, I had an addition to my web tattoo. A tiny spider. Long black legs banded in orange protruding from a narrow black body faintly marked with vertical orange lines.

"A male black widow," his woman told me as she worked. "It survives only if it is taken early and placed in isolation."

"Early?"

"Before birth is best. Directly from the egg sac. If it

grows to adult unprotected, it will die immediately after first mating. That is its destiny, to die."

"Every time?" I asked, flash-thinking of Cherry for reasons I didn't understand. Not then.

"Yes."

"So, if isolated at birth, what is its destiny, then?"

"If it doesn't leave the isolation, *still* to die. Only to die."

"But what if it doesn't? What if it grows to full size and *then* leaves, leaves without mating? Does its destiny change?"

"A spider whose destiny is to die has no need of the ability to spin a web," she answered. "So if the spider who can only grow in isolation escapes, what must it do then?"

"Walk?"

"Yes," the old woman said, touching the new addition to my tattoo. "And, remember, the kinetics spell you purchased works only on objects. For anything else...."

Weeks passed before I accepted that I could never find the path to the money by working the Sector. Once I reached that acceptance, I was ready to go. All tools packed. Except those I'd have to return to the Synthetic Woman for.

"You have the pre-paid words for me?" I asked. Not doubting, collecting.

"Yes. One to cross; two to return."

"I meet the Driver in the launch circle?

"Yes."

"And to return?"

"The Poison Tree. The same one you—"

"—I remember. Just return to the Poison Tree and say the words?"

"Both words. You cannot come back without my child."

"What if she's—"

"—Then say both words, still. But why would—"

"I don't know what's in the Pure Zone. Neither do you. But in all places, there are always merchants. Perhaps I might bargain to have her brought over first ... I might have to stay until I fulfill that contract."

"That's possible, possibly. But if you cannot bring me my child, or have her brought to me, you must bring me proof of her death. And if that is all you bring, expect interrogation."

I sipped the dry-iced drink she served. Radiated my patience.

"How old was your child when she was taken?" I finally asked her.

"A baby."

"A baby could be a day old. Or a year."

For answer, she just shrugged.

"How long ago, taken?" I asked, trying to find another path.

"Years."

I waited through three cigarettes and one drink refill. Nothing.

"A baby could be worth money in the City," I tried. "Big money to the right people."

She didn't react.

"So why are you so certain your child is in the Pure Zone?"

"Because I know of all those who transport across the Membrane. Just as I know spells cannot cross it. The words I give you are only messages that travel, not spells. Those, I know you have already purchased...."

"Are you sure the child is even alive?" I asked, ignoring her probe.

She shrugged again.

"You have photos?"

She tapped one perfect temple.

I waited. Finally, she started to speak.

But the baby she described could have been anyone's. Or everyone's. I couldn't be sure when the Synthetic Woman had all the work done to her body, but that didn't matter. I knew her mutated DNA wouldn't be a match for any other human's, not anymore.

I found the three-story steel silo that housed the club easily enough. Watched *Apex Predator* swirl in pulsing red/white/black neon through the artificial haze for an hour before I entered.

Inside was a cave of sound—hissing steam and pounding punk. The decor was gears, all turning in connecto-counterpoint to the throb of industrial music. Communication was only by gesture. Anywhere outside one of the soundproof dome-booths, conversation was impossible.

The tiny stage was lit by a single blush-spot. A maybe-Asian girl with ice-kohl eyes stepped into its glow. Her costume was a black bridal dress, cut high above her knees, black mesh stockings, black heels with gold soles. A black pillbox hat with matching half-veil. And a wide black band around her neck.

A suicide singer, always the headliner in such places. One of the reasons City-born cross the Membrane to

visit—suicide singers are banned on their side, like so many other things people think they want. Once tasted, abstinence is no longer an option.

The music slid into a dull throb, punctuated with cardiogram beeps.

Her voice was breathy. Not sexy, oxygen-deprived.

It hurts to be alone
It's so hard to love a stone
And such pain to be alive
Sometimes

It hurts to cry
But it doesn't hurt to die
Don't you want to help me try?

She floated delicately off the stage. Her movements were tender, as if she was going to walk over the bodies of people she cared about in those stiletto heels. The suicide singer wafted through the room. She never went beyond forcefield-flirting, never touching or allowing a touch.

I lit a cigarette. Maybe it was the glow that brought her to my booth. "Want to bring me there?" she asked, handing me a pneumatic bulb connected by a tube to the black band around her neck. I knew the game then. A

compression collar. I'd heard about them, never seen one before.

I shook my head "no." she ignored the gesture, closing her eyes so only the kohl showed.

"Mind the dial," she whispered. I tried to hand back the bulb.

"You *have* to," she whispered. "They're watching."

I didn't waste breath on asking her who she meant. "A trade," I said, very softly. "I'll pay; they'll see me doing that. But you have to trade."

Without waiting for a response, I squeezed the bulb. The dial moved. At "2," she put her hands behind her back and thrust her chest out bravely, as if facing a firing squad.

The music stayed monotonous, but its beat was thicker, more insistent.

At "4," her legs trembled.

At "5" she dropped to her knees.

At "6" her face fell into my lap.

I pulled the red tablecloth over her, left it in place as she finished.

I lit another smoke, let it simmer in the ashtray as she rearranged us under the tablecloth. Then I pulled it away, snapped the release on the compression collar, and held a gold coin out with my right hand. Only a few seconds passed, then she crawled out and took it in her teeth.

As she disappeared back into the darkness, the music shifted again, back to the industrial pounding, a chorus of pile-drivers at work.

I waited through two more cigarettes. Then I stood up and walked over to Booth Six. When I closed the curtains, the glass top of the table lit up with the message I'd traded for.

The Sector is a maze of steps. No elevators, no escalators. From street level, some steps go up, some down. One way is dangerous, another is deadly. Here, the least mobile are the most to be feared. The immobiles thread out to the mobiles, spiders at the center of their webs.

Being the most dangerous doesn't always make you the most safe. Those spiders don't have error margins. Hitting the wrong target can make them one. Missing some targets guarantees that.

That's what had brought me to prison. I had been closing the distance to the center when a Dark White fringe player was dropped for something he did to his own

child. He qualified for Special Handling off the second six-pack the cops showed him.

"You recognize anyone?" they'd started with.

"I recognize *all* of them," he finished the conversation, dropping his straight flush on the table.

His lawyer made the deal.

A few weeks later, they came for me. Another few days, I made mine.

It was two years and eight months before my Judas came in. The people who got word to me gave me his new name—his reward for informing—and where he was locked. Their message was clear: they knew the only pictures *I'd* ever recognized had been righteous. Never mug shots, only morgue shots.

You can name the dead, but you can't hurt them.

I'd earned my name many years before I earned my ink, before I tried every way I could think of to cross the Membrane ... and stay there. But I only had the one skill, and it wasn't a big earner.

"It's a new game," Mighty said. Said it the way he said everything, packing the air with low-voiced intensity. "Hottest thing going," he assured me. He'd gone by "Mighty" since we were kids. The over/under was top-

heavy that he'd named himself.

"I'm not going in the box again," I told him. "Box" was just a word for "locked in." Not always a ring. Sometimes it was a room, sometimes a pit, sometimes just a narrow tunnel. Tunnels didn't bring in the top money, because the crowds can't watch the fight, only witness the outcome.

Paying to see which man walked out.

No referee needed, because there's no rules. They do search each man before it starts. A full probe, even the fingernails for razor-shards. But once they lock you in, there's no such thing as cheating.

Mighty was an expert at wrapping the scrotum. Some go max for protection, but that hampers agility. So some go too light, and that hampers survival. Mighty had the perfect touch.

"Why not?" he'd demanded. "The box, that's your home. Last time, we made—"

"I don't know what *you* made," I cut him off. With what I'd gotten out of it, I would have to fight every day for years and *still* be way short of what I needed. This being the Sector, Mighty had never asked how much I needed, never mind what for.

That last fight had been a bad one. The other man cast a smaller silhouette than me, so I'd expected him to be

faster. But I'd guessed wrong. He wasn't fast at all—his weapon was pain tolerance.

The fight itself was fast—mine always are. I fired a ridge hand to the juncture of his neck and clavicle, but all he did was grunt and ram his shaved head at me. I reached inside, grabbed his thumb, cranked it full as I brought an elbow into his temple. He blinked a couple of times, shifted into full limbic mode and rammed again, screaming. I fishhooked him. Didn't change anything, he kept coming. It wasn't until I got my thumb deep into a socket and corkscrewed all the way to the pop-out that he went down, clawing at his face as if he could replace the eye he'd lost. I stomped on his Adam's apple like it was a concrete roach.

Mighty must have seen all that in the look I gave him. "This is new, I'm telling you," he'd said, dropping his voice like he had some big secret to share. "No rounds. No judges. It's going to be bar-fight format."

"You mean bottles and—"

"—Nothing like that. How long does a bar fight last? That's the key to this one. Every match is sixty seconds, max. In an eight-foot Lexan cube. No place to hide. That's your meat, Carbon. You're a blitz-fighter, not some cardio-freak."

Mighty prided himself on being an analyst, but he

couldn't see things from the inside. Not *my* inside. When I fight, there's no speed. It's like some force drops a clear-syrup curtain over everything—turns it all into slow motion. I can see it coming like it had made a reservation. It's nothing I was taught ... that's just the way it happens. Every time.

"There's potions for speed," is all I said.

"Those?" he sneered. "Everyone knows they're lunar. Even when they work, all they do is make everything move fast inside you ... don't do nothing for your strikes. Only time to use speed-up is *between* rounds. And like I told you, this new thing, they *got* no rounds."

"So how do they—"

"—It's elimination-deal, get me? You lose, you're out. If both men're still awake at the end, that's a tie. And ties mean you lose ... you *both* lose, get it? Final winner takes the purse, the *whole* purse."

"How much is the—"

"—Depends on how many ante. It's a full Tiger to come in, and the house matches the total. That's why no side-bets allowed; they run it parimutuel, see? So the bettors, they set the odds, but the house sets the take-out."

"I don't know...."

"I'll put up the Tiger," Mighty said. "And I'll bet heavy with the house, too. We split down the middle. You could

clear two, three hundred, easy."

"Or die."

"Come on! Getting put to sleep, that's the only risk."

"You don't go square on the split this time, that's not *your* only risk," I told him.

I ended up with one hundred and ninety-one Tigers. A tiny piece of what I needed. It took months for me to heal, and cost most of what I'd earned. Cost more, actually. Pain can stretch a split-second into an hour inside you, but all the currency on earth can't move time in the other direction.

Mighty knew lots of ways to gamble. In the Sector, you can bet on anything. Only miniatures are permitted to be kept, and the lizard races are a big favorite. They never kill the losers. Instead, they sell them to smugglers—in the City, keeping a micro-dragon is illegal, so they're worth a serious piece of money. Money enough to buy goods to bring back across the Membrane. That's how things are. How they've always been.

A month after I was healed, I was down to credit.

I had one more fight—not the new format, just a single one-on-one. That cleared my debts. I had to do that to keep my word. I had to keep my word to keep my name.

Then I was done with the box—everything I had went into chasing the Dark White cache.

I walked the Sector without concern for the City police. They had learned long before that the streets are too narrow for anything but electric bikes, and those can't be armored. Every once in a while, the City sends road crews across the Membrane to widen the streets, but garbage always flies down faster than it can be cleared. Retro-erosion, with the native species always reclaiming the beach.

I bought a short loaf of dragon-tail bread from a street vendor. Walked further down the twisted lane and handed it to a woman standing behind a heavy vat of onion-and-ginseng stew. She pulled off the spikes, scooped out their insides, and filled the created pockets with her concoction, placing each one carefully in a cardboard carry-tray. Watching my face for approval, she added a small wooden bowl of watermelon radishes and broadleaf spinach, then sprinkled it with bok choy and pearl onions. I paid her and sat down on a metal barrel, slowly chewing.

A boy on a trike came by with clear bottles of colored liquids. I took a gray one, paid him with two of the filled crusts. He racked the crusts in his basket and watched quietly as I sipped the crushed bilberry and finished my meal. Then he took the empty bottle, the wooden bowl and the cardboard tray from me and recycled away.

My hands rested on the chimney surround, palms facing in, forming a *trompe l'oeil* to the teenager I faced.

"You sure you're quick enough?" I said, as I touched the first two fingers of my left hand to the soot on the chimney's spout and showed him the dark tips. "Before you decide, look at your face in the mirror."

"Why would I do that?"

"To be sure," I told him.

He scanned his face in the hand mirror, as satisfied with his own reflection as he was sure of the steel in his belt.

"Okay?" I said.

"Sure," he said, twisting his mouth. "They don't call me 'Stick' because I'm thin, old man."

"You must be right," I agreed. "Now look in the mirror again."

He staggered back from the reflection. "How did...?"

I didn't answer him, letting the twin tracks of soot trailing from cheekbone to jaw line speak for me.

"Okay *now?*" I asked.

He held his hands away from his belt, as if to assure me he wouldn't reach for the weapon that had earned him his name.

Then he started to talk.

"Here's the key," Stick said, his confidence returning as he realized it wasn't his day to die. "Anything you can think of, anything you could ever imagine ... no matter what it is, *somebody* wants it. Think of something you'd never do. *Never* do, no matter how much you got paid, okay? The thing to know is this: there's always someone who'll pay *to* do that."

I kept looking, patient. Finally found the door where Stick had promised I'd find the de-gens.

There was only one of them. His face was a post-mortem display of blunt-instrument assault: stitch scars, acid burns, off-center nose, one missing eyebrow, jagged teeth.

No point watching that place for more. That's how the Sector works. The heads-on-stakes message from one tribe would keep the other away. A sight like that can spook a man ... even in de-gen form.

I found the supply store easy enough. The proprietor sells boots to tourist skinheads—he's afraid not to. But he's fussy about his merchandise. He only allows in-person purchases. Tells them he has to make sure they fit— professional pride. He's already marked the heel of each pair and keeps a record, cross-indexed to a surreptitiously snapped photograph of every buyer. That record is his secret, a treasure never to be unearthed. No one knows why he keeps it, or even that it exists.

No one is *supposed* to know, anyway.

So I didn't even have to offer currency to get him to show it to me.

But for all the leads it provided, every page could have been blank.

Potions work best when the purest chemicals combine with virgin botanicals. The chemist I went back to never

seemed to age. I had, but he recognized me easily enough. Ultimate toxins are always without marks: never an odor, taste, or color ... like the catabolic steroids used to slow-rot muscles. He creates poisons custom brewed to an individual's blood type. If you want the product, you have to bring him a sample.

I watched the alley mouth. The hitman was stylish. The man hunting him had no style. No custom clothes, no jewelry. What he wore was Patience. It would take as long as it took.

When the hitman moved, I was in his wake. By the time I was done, I knew he wasn't holding anything back.

But his info was as useful as a sextant in the Sector.

Before I went under into Dark White, even before I got my papers as a Cross-Membrane PI, I did his kind of work myself. Across the Membrane, killing for money is no different than shoveling coal. A task. You work until you're done. Then you start over.

I only took certain jobs. Always screened deep. When a man's killer is welcome at his funeral, it's because there

aren't many mourners. That's why I specialized in de-gens.

His lecture hall was a red-candled basement.

"When someone tells you something, you have to know how they know what they know, so you can know if what they know is a true know or a false no."

The lunatic gestured for "Hold your applause, please," with his palsied hands, halting his run-on just long enough to confirm that his audience—me—was enraptured. Then he rolled on:

"The basement windows are casement windows. Behind the glass are the debasement windows. The trophy-takers feed the money-makers."

The lunatic was speaking C-base—the code that writes code. Any other language would lack the reassurance of ritual, would fail to keep the voices at bay. C-base is a worm program. Once it enters, it runs at warp—even if the quarry carries a tablet, it won't blink the tracking cursor. The only software that works on psychos is pattern recognition, and the darkest of those rewrite their patterns too quickly to unravel a solid prediction. A good C-base decoder can tell you where a psycho's been, but not where he's going.

I knew the amulet was in there someplace, but I didn't have time to search. So I amateur-trashed the place, filling my grab-bag with random goods that looked like pawn bait. I stayed just long enough to plant the cross-beamed fisheye dots, and went back to my high-story post.

The second he entered his apartment, he went frantically to work. Not even wasting time to gasp at the carnage to his nest, he flung aside some throw rugs and started madly tapping on the floor tiles. A minute later, a lid slid open and he took out the amulet. The wireless feed was perfect. I watched as he pocketed the amulet and headed for the door.

I had him before he found a new hiding place.

I traded the amulet for the rest of what I needed.

But I still couldn't make the formula work.

I'd read all the signs I could, staying patient, doing the math. Without the killer the cops wanted, they wouldn't let me off the leash, so I couldn't hope to track the Dark White money. But I had another road: the Synthetic Woman. If I got her job done, she'd be good on her word. Or call in her assassins. All I had was words. The cops

promised I could run free if I turned up the killer for them. But even if they kept their word, I'd be running on a carousel unless the Synthetic Woman kept hers.

A gamble inside a gamble, a fool's throw of loaded dice.

But the other choice was to die without trying.

So I put all my gear together, and checked for balance. Then I climbed down to the pavement, found the tunnel I needed, and headed for the river.

It was clear nearly all the way to the end. I had to use one of the Frankensteins to finish the trip.

"My contract's not with you, it's with the Money Men, understand?"

"I do," I answered, solemnly as a wedding vow. As I had been warned by the shamans, I was aging with every mile closer to the border, my speech-style shifting to match my face.

"I'm not getting into any duel," the driver said, trying to weave a thread of threat into his voice. His visuals intentionally provided little information: body was age-blurring fat, eyes shielded by black goggles, hands covered in padded mesh gloves of the same color. When his passenger—me—remained silent, he added, "Don't even try," In a flabby underscore.

"I issued no challenge," I assured him. The driver glanced over quickly, seeing only a featureless man, except for the curved patch of impure white across his left cheekbone. His instant assessment—*radiation burn*—was unvoiced. The driver was not a man who shared what he believed to be valuable.

When we got close enough to the border to test one of the spells I'd purchased, I touched the pocket on the front of my gray canvas jacket. I felt it churn, extracted a cigarette wrapped in dark yellow leaf.

"No smoking in my machine," the driver's tone carried what he meant to be a note of warning.

I took a deep drag.

"You're not going to light that."

I exhaled.

"Wait! What is that thing?"

His question was a fraud, not seeking an answer. I closed my eyes.

"This your first time?" the driver asked, his tone clearly conveying that he knew the answer.

I didn't respond. If I told him that I knew the way, he'd only ask more questions. If I told him I didn't, he'd spew a string of lies.

I'd never been this side of the river before, but I knew the route and I could read the markers. A man I'd been close to Inside had been across three times ... or so he'd said. "It isn't a place you want to stay," he told me, one day as we were walking the yard together. "No matter how good it looks, staying there, that's always the wrong decision." Considering where we were at the time, I wondered if he'd made the right one.

Together was the only way to walk the yard—actually, walk the oval track that circled the yard. Walking across the yard itself was a tightrope act, not something you did unless you had a safe spot to go to. Or bad intentions.

The other man carried the same ink I did. Despite what we all called ourselves, that ink didn't make us brothers ... but it did give us enemies in common. Others shared our skin color, but that didn't necessarily make them enemies to our enemies ... just targets.

That other man was walking an endless loop, and not the one in the yard. Escape plots always bubbled the foul prison air, but all those plots were waiting for a train at a station without tracks. Escape fantasies circulated like bats in daylight: out of their element, confused. Too much competing noise to get a signal ... so they never touched down.

And never fed.

For me to know if the dead speak, I'd have to rely on those who claim to hear them. To truly know, I'd have to die. The man walking with me was the closest I could come to that.

Me, I had an out-time set. I couldn't be sure when the gate would unlock, not exactly, but it *would* happen, even if the people I'd made the deal with broke their word about a quickie parole. None of that was in the future of the man I walked with, so he shared what he knew. A safety play, a maybe-move. Maybe, someday, I'd need what he knew. What he was sharing. And if I ever did, maybe I would remember where I'd gotten it.

That's what I promised him. I don't know if he was counting on the reputation I'd built up in there, or if word had reached him from Outside. Maybe he just figured he had nothing to lose. Maybe believing me gave him something he didn't have before.

The real maybe was this: I'd never been on this side of the river, but the man I'd left Inside had told me enough to draw maps from memory.

If he remembered. If he hadn't been lying.

"You know I'm not crossing the border. Even in daylight. They told you all that, right? This here's a Cargo

Car. I move product to the line, never past it. That's always in the contract, every time."

I opened my eyes. Said nothing.

"Look, like I said when you first got in, the deal isn't with you, okay? There's two packages. One I make disappear, the other I drive to the border. *To* the border, understand? You, you're one of the packages. Like any other package, nothing special. That's what I do, I move packages," he said, trying for a hard voice as he glanced meaningfully at the cage which took up most of the back of the heavy wagon.

"Once you get out, we're done. For now, I mean. I see you again, I don't see you again, makes no difference to me," the driver said, nearly exhausting his supply of self-reassurance.

"Yeah, they told me about you," he went on, still trying for calm, gesturing as if brushing away an annoying fly. "I heard. Tricks and all. You do the kind of work I do, you see stunts like that smooth-hand stuff of yours all the time. They don't change nothing."

"Stop being afraid," I told him.

"I'm not..." the driver began, deliberately letting his voice trail off, inviting me to fill in the empty space.

I declined with my silence.

After some unmeasured, no-meaning time, the driver flicked a toggle switch, activating infrared beams. He adjusted a lever on his goggles, enabling him to read the cracked-concrete roadway. Another switch produced a full head-up display in the windshield: speed, road temperature, a count-down clock, and descending kilometers-to-destination. The dash held a ribbon of images, a 360-degree viewer. The driver was a man who believed in business investments.

"Less than thirty, now," he snapped.

"As you say."

"I know this road like I know my own tunnel. I couldn't go past it, anyway; they only sold me four cells of juice. I'll show you where—"

"—Just stop wherever you have to," I interrupted.

"I didn't mean the drop-off, okay? The contract is for two packages, remember? You and the gun."

"I can't touch the pistol," I said. "Not on this side. They would have told you this."

"Yeah, that's what they said. I don't see why—"

"—Yours not to see," I chopped off the sentence, switching to a formal, measured tone. "Yours only to say. And the contract speaks your words. You are not a partner

in this. You agreed to perform tasks for a payment. You received that payment. You accepted it. Nothing more is due to you."

"I wasn't asking for nothing more."

"Answering questions, that would be more."

"Hey! There's no reason to get all big-deal, okay? I'm not your damn butler, I drive a Cargo Car. Wasn't for my skills, you couldn't even get to the border, am I right?"

"No."

The driver opened his mouth to speak, then decided against it.

A few minutes later, the driver pressed his palm against the console between the bucket seats. The cover slid open. His gloved hand reached inside and came out with the used Frankenstein—I'd turned the virgin one into currency before I'd ever entered the tunnel. A tap on the steering wheel's hub and his window zipped down.

"When we get to the next bridge," he announced.

"No."

"No? Look, you don't know this route. Next bridge, it's the one they call The Kangol. You know what that is?"

"A kepi," I said. "For a different army."

"Huh?"

"Just keep driving."

"Look, I'm trying to tell you something here. When we cross the bridge, the left side, the water under there's deep enough to cover a high-rise. This crappy road narrows down to one-way for the crossing, so I can slide up close. That's where—"

"—Your knowledge is old knowledge," I told him, staying very formal. "Old, so you respect it. But it is *shared* knowledge. By too many, for too long."

"Just talk plain, all right?"

"This, then: so many weapons have been tossed off what you call The Kangol that a stalactite of deadly metal has grown up. It is now so close to the surface that each new deposit sets off sparks."

"Like it's all-of-a-sudden shallow?"

"As a dry creek bed."

"I'd like to see that."

"On your next trip in daylight, maybe you will."

"So what am I supposed to with this gun? I got paid to dump it. You know all about that, remember?"

"When we get closer to the border."

"Not *too* close, okay? You know what happens to anyone who tries to bring a gun over."

"No."

"No? Come on, *everybody* knows."

"Everybody *hears*. Just as you heard that the best place to dump a firearm was under The Kangol."

"We're maybe five-six minutes out, now. And we still haven't dumped the—"

"—Do you know the Poison Tree?"

"Sure. All the haulers know it. First warning."

"All right, then. When your sensors pick it up, that will be close enough."

"I'm not leaving any gun that close to the border. We've got to—"

"—Not when you reach it, when you *see* it. That's where you stop."

An impossibly thick tree sat in a swampy patch to the right side of the road. Its nest-of-snakes root system resembled healthy mangrove, but its branches were as bare as a fire survivor's. In the beam from the car's infrareds, the trunk fluoresced into the cyanotic blue of a fatally ill child.

The driver expertly steered to a spot on solid ground. "Here's how we're going to do this: You get out; take the

gun with you. I'll put it back in the bag myself; you won't have to touch it. You didn't want it off The Kangol, that was your call. But a contract's still a contract."

I gave him silence.

"Hey man, you heard me. I said a contract's still a contract. Sometimes I haul a dozen at once ... plenty of room in the back for the kids they send. I got it all set up with air filtration and water—I'm a professional. So, no little tricks, now. Remember, I'm the only one who can take you back."

"Sure," I said.

The driver's unspoken questions hovered behind me as I exited the car. Carrying the mesh bag containing the Frankenstein in one hand, I treaded carefully on my approach to the Poison Tree. Kneeling, I placed the bag in the marshy water. It slowly sank from sight, a trail of bubbles marking its descent to depths beyond reach. As it disappeared, a copper-banded bamboo box popped to the surface. I took it with both hands. It was unlocked. I transferred its contents to my duffel, nodded a bow to the spirits, and returned the box to its home.

As I began to move past the tree, the driver suddenly wheeled into a snap-spin, throwing off a shower of dirt,

twigs, and leaves as the Cargo Car shot back the way it had come. He jammed the accelerator to the floor, his mouth set in a hard line as if to freeze his shivering lips.

The first spell I spoke let me see it as clearly as if projected on a screen:

As the car crossed The Kangol, its engine changed pitch.

Off-market products are always traded on trust—counterfeit fuel cells are indistinguishable from those properly charged. The driver cursed. He reached for the fresh-cell toggle as the dash lights blinked once mockingly, then disappeared.

The car went dark.

As night fully enveloped, the driver would finally stop walking, his expectation that another of his kind would pass fading down to tiny tendrils of dying hopes. Soon, even those hopes would be as empty as the cells he had purchased.

And he'd be as abandoned-to-hell as the children he hauled.

I walked for the four hours I'd been told, using the time to acclimate my lungs. I could *feel* the air, it was so clogged with oxygen. I could only guess at the time—clocks wouldn't work on this side. But measuring time without clocks, that was something prison was good at teaching.

My lungs expanded as the O$_2$ enrichment deepened. The cones in my eyes narrowed to accommodate the crystal-pixel light, just as they had expanded while I was in Iso.

I kept walking until I saw the first sign.

The child sat forlornly atop a war-ravaged length of stone. It was all that remained of a missile shelter never worthy of such a lofty title.

A little girl, somewhere between six and eight years old, I guessed. Once sunflower blonde and china blue, her hair and eyes were now colors never present at birth. She was wearing a pink princess dress over a white petticoat and black ballet slippers with white anklets, dressed for a party.

Her eyes had vacuumed the earth's sadness, holding it hostage for a ransom never to be paid.

"I have no one to play with," she said, plucking at the

hem of her dress. Not "No one will play with me," the Sector word-signal that others were lurking somewhere in her Survival Space.

My eyes stayed on hers. I had already registered the opening in the wall of rubble behind her, the danger-dance of its shifting shadows.

"Will *you* play with me?" the child asked.

"I'm looking for someone," I said by way of answer.

"I could help you look," she offered, brightly.

"Back in there?"

"Oh, yes! It's nice in there. Not hot, like out here. We could—"

"—You go," I told her. "You go back there. Ask them to come out and talk to me."

"But there's nobody in—"

"—Yes, there is," I said, keeping my voice gentle, just above a whisper. "I'm not angry with you. I know you're only doing what you're supposed to do, what you have been taught. Go back there. Tell them I want to talk. Tell them to come to the portal; I'll meet them there. Tell them I have currency. Will you do that?"

"I'm not supposed to talk out here. And never for long. I have to—"

"—I know. You're supposed to bring me back with you. *Through* the portal. But I won't do that."

"I don't have anyone to—"

"—play with. Yes, I know. If you bring them past the portal to talk to me, I'll change that," I promised softly. "All of that." I stepped back and stared at the shadows, waiting. "Don't listen to words," I said to the child. "Words can lie. *Feel* the truth."

The little girl slowly climbed down from the stone. She looked at the strange man one last time, then stepped off into the shadows.

I waited, motionless. Felt the sun's stabbing rays pass painlessly through me, leaving the warmth of Patience behind. When the child waved to me, I walked to where crumbled stone had formed a random portal.

They stepped out toward me. Three of them: two females and a male. The taller female was wrapped in a shawl large enough to conceal many weapons. The smaller one was wrapped as well, in a body suit of what looked like molded pink mesh. The male stood a half-step behind them, hands clasped in front of him. As they moved closer, I could see those hands were wrapped, too ... in weaves of flesh-colored wire.

"You have currency?" the taller female demanded.

"I *am* currency," I told her.

"What will you do, then?"

"Whatever you want done. But only if you can tell me where to find someone I'm looking for."

She shifted her posture. "Ah. You are a seeker, then?"

"Sure," I shrugged, making it clear that self-attached labels were meaningless.

"Then we will tell you only the truth," the smaller female said, arching her back and smiling at me. "Do you want to come with me?"

I flowed toward her seductive invitation, reaching out my right hand. As she opened her arms, I spun on my front foot and chopped at her throat with the edge of my left. She dropped while the crack of her hyoid bone still echoed in the surrounding stone.

The male clenched his wire-wrapped fists and slogged forward. I could see the horseshoe jaw implant, a heavy shelf of metal that would deflect any blow, even one from a club. I slammed a palm underneath that chin. The implant shifted with the strike. The male screamed, clutching at his face. When I moved in, he wrapped his orangutan arms around me, still shrieking. But he'd left one of my hands free. I found the pulse in his neck and pressed until it stopped.

The larger female never moved, watching as if this was a movie and she wanted to see how it turned out. Then she

rushed fearlessly, claws extended. I snatched her shawl with both hands and turned in the same motion, using the momentum to fling her into the jagged wall.

I scanned quickly. There were no more of them. So I finished what there was.

The words of an ancient prison-mystic came back. He'd been locked down so long there was no paper on him anywhere. Word was, he could leave whenever he wanted.

His words: *Had they not promised to tell me the truth, I would not have known their truth.*

He had been talking about his interrogators. The ones he'd outlived. His words echoed as I stood between the portal I had refused to enter and the bodies of the corpses I had created.

After a while, the child came out of the shadows.

As we passed by where she had been posted on the low concrete wall, the child suddenly cried out: "Wait! You *have* to wait. I need my treasure."

"You can never return," I warned her. "This place is well-designed for its purpose. It will bring others who want to use it the same way."

"Not back there. It's *here.* Out here. I never bring it inside," the child said, calming as she saw me halt. She

dropped to her knees and began to remove a series of small stones, working carefully, as if the precise order of removal was the combination to a safe.

"Mine!" she shouted in triumph, holding up a small book wrapped in what had once been oxblood leather.

The road was hard-packed earth, deeply rutted. It snaked through what might once have been a village, now a ruin of stone, iron, brick, and steel, sprinkled with resurrections of rusted tin and pitted aluminum that had been fashioned into now-abandoned housing. The only glass was shards randomly attached to the last structures, some of it backed with foil to create a mirror effect.

"Where are the solars?" I asked the child.

"We're not to know that."

"Why?"

"Because it's a secret. And it's a deadly offense to know a secret."

I knew about the secrets of such children, so I reached into my duffel, closing my hand into a fist. When I opened the hand, a sun-yellow ball appeared.

"What is that?"

"Food. It is called 'yellowcake,' because it comes from the ground, but not in a form you could eat. It must have

certain ingredients added to transform it first."

"It's cake?"

"Yes."

"Is it good?"

"The taste, you are asking?"

"I ... guess."

"Taste is inside every person."

"I don't know what that means."

"It means what tastes good to one person might not taste the same to another."

"To *you*, then. Does it taste good to you?"

"It's food. When you're hungry, food tastes good."

"I'm hungry. I'm always hungry. But...."

I extended my hand. "Pull a piece from the yellowcake."

"Why?"

"So it will be your choice."

"But if I don't want—"

"—Not for you, for me. You don't trust. That's good. That's smart. It doesn't make me angry. I'm a stranger—there's no reason to trust me."

The child tentatively touched the yellowcake. "It's warm."

"It's always warm when fresh," I told her. "Now take a piece. Not for yourself, remember. For me."

The child pushed two fingers into the yellowcake, pulled the fingers toward her thumb, extracted a sample, and reached up to give it to me.

I put it into my mouth, chewed gently, swallowed.

The child watched, waiting.

When I began to walk again, the child skipped quickly to regain her place by my side.

"Isn't there some for me?" she asked.

"When you are satisfied."

"I don't know what you mean."

"You saw me eat a piece of the yellowcake. Don't you want to wait and see if that causes any ill effects?"

"You mean, if it's like poison or something?"

"Yes."

"Oh, I already know it's not," she said, confidently.

"How do you know?"

"Because I saw what you did to ... them. If you wanted to hurt me, or make me do something, you could, couldn't you?"

"Yes."

"So you wouldn't need any ... yellowcake, yes? ... you wouldn't need anything like that."

"Not to do the things you said, no."

"Can I have the cake, now?"

When I flexed my palm the ball of yellowcake grew to

twice its former size. The child took it in both hands and carefully nibbled as she walked.

"It's so good!"

"You were hungry," I told her, keeping a promise.

We halted by a pool of rainwater which had collected in a hollowed-out slab of rock.

"It might not be safe," the child warned, her voice heavy with the gravity of knowledge. "There's probably no solar to purify it. Not until we get back to where people are."

"People are here," I told her. "You saw their housing as we passed. It was people who fashioned this rain-collector."

"Oh."

I took a cup from my duffel. It was gray metal, with a black handle. I scooped it full, and handed it to the child.

"I...."

"You want me to drink it first? Like with the yellowcake?"

"I guess that's stupid, isn't it?"

"The first time, it was smart. Now, that's up to you. But if you want to go through that routine every time, you'll always be the last to eat."

"I *am* always the last to eat."

"That was with those other people."

"The ones you killed."

I didn't answer what hadn't been a question, just took a long drink. Then I refilled the cup and handed it to the child. She took it without hesitation.

"This tastes good!"

"You were thirsty."

"Is that how it works? The same as with food?"

"Everything works that way."

"I don't understand."

"Yes, you do. You just don't have the words."

"I have words. I have *lots* of words. See!" she said, holding up the little book she had retrieved.

"A dictionary?"

"That's what a word-book is called, yes. A man gave it to me."

"When you—"

"—Oh, no," she said hurriedly. "He was a very smart man. Like you. He knew what was waiting inside the portal. Where I was to bring him. He knew right away. He said, 'I am not a warrior, child, but I still have value for you. Only for you, never for those who hide in wait.' Then he said, 'I am a troubadour. And this is my work.' And he dropped this book on the ground. His hands were below

the wall, and the others couldn't have seen, even if they were watching. Then he just walked away."

"How did you manage to hide your book?"

"It took a long time. They expect me to climb off my post—that's what Gret called where I had to sit every day, my post—a few times whenever they sent me out. When I'd have to ... you know."

My silence was sufficient to tell her that I did know.

"It took forever to hide it, it seemed like. At first I was scared."

"That they would see you?"

"No. I knew they couldn't. I knew they never come far past the portal. I heard Gret tell them they never could go too far into the light. If they did that, then they would be bad. If the wrong people saw them, they could all get killed."

"Then they would be bad?" I asked her. Puzzled, trying not to show it.

"Yes! If they stayed back there, they couldn't be bad, because no one could kill them. Am I saying that right?"

"I don't know. If they couldn't see you, what frightened you about hiding your book?"

"Rain. I had nothing to wrap it in. And I knew if I tore my dress, they'd burn me. Until I got it safe behind the stones, I was scared the paper would get all rotten. I knew

I needed my words."

"Words aren't to have; words are to use."

"Now you're saying I'm stupid, aren't you?"

"No," I said, starting to see, the truth emerging like a developing photograph. "But that's what you expect when you speak, isn't it? To be called stupid."

"That's the way...."

I let my silence encourage her.

"Oh! I was going to say, that's the way it ... works. *That's* what you meant. Before. When you said I knew, but I ... didn't know how to say it. *That's* it. Am I right? Am I ... correct?"

"You're close. But you can't use those ... people who trained you as a reference point."

"A what?"

"An example of how things are. How things are supposed to be. You're not stupid. So, if you're not stupid, what does that make people who *call* you stupid?"

She spent a few seconds in thought, then suddenly burst out: "It makes *them* stupid?"

"If they truly believed what they said, yes, they would be stupid. But they didn't really believe you were stupid. They called you names because the names hurt you. They made you feel helpless—a child with no choices."

"Children don't *have* choices."

"How do you know that? Because those people told you?"

"Yes. And because children who try to make choices are bad. They make bad things happen to them."

"There were other children back in that cave?"

"No. Not anymore. There used to be. Two boys, and a girl. Besides me, I mean. But they were bigger. Older. And when they tried to ... when they tried to do anything bad, it would always end the same. I saw a lot of things that happened. When I was very little. By the time I was old enough to perform at my post, the others were all gone."

"Escaped?"

"They got killed. I didn't want to get killed."

"So you were afraid of those people, but you didn't *believe* them. You were afraid of them, but now they're gone. So now comes the truth: You *do* have choices."

"Are you sure?"

"When I walked away, you walked with me. Wasn't that a choice? *Your* choice?"

"I ... don't know."

"Did I force you to walk with me?"

"No, but.... Wait! What else could I do? I don't know how to get food. I only know how to...."

"I know. But you could have walked away in another direction. You might have found food on your own."

"I *could* have, you know. I was ... lying, before. But, this, this isn't a lie. I know a lot of things. I went with you because I knew you would never hurt me."

I scooped another cup of water and held it to my lips, raising my eyebrows in a question. The child reached across and took the cup from my hands.

"That water, it's pure. We made it that way. So there's a tax on it."

The speaker was a squat man with an asymmetrical skull and hands disproportionately large for his body.

"What is the tax?" I asked.

"Toss your pack over here. I have to see what you have, first."

"What I have, I need."

"That's not my problem. You used our water, so—"

"—We used no water of yours."

"Then what was in that cup? Before you drank from it?"

"The reservoir you created is full to the brim. Why not look for yourself?"

The tax collector approached cautiously, his eyes never leaving my duffel, as if all danger to him was in there. When he was standing next to the rock, he risked a quick

glance. The water level was past the brim, spilling over the rock in gentle rivulets.

"As though it just poured for a week," he muttered.

I gave him silence.

"Who are you?" the tax collector demanded.

"Just a traveler," I said. "One who means you no harm."

"Is that right?"

"Yes, it is," the child piped up. "*I* don't mean you any harm, either."

The tax collector patted the rock, as if it would transmit some message. Finally, he said, "You can't stay here, you know. There's a—"

"—Yes. Another of your taxes. We'll be on our way soon."

"Well, if you come back...."

I gave him more silence.

"Was that a bad man?" the child asked.

"The tax collector?"

"Yes. Was he bad?"

"I don't know."

"He *looked* bad."

"You mean the shape of his head?"

"No. I'm not dumb. I know where that comes from. The water, isn't that true?"

"The water? We drank the water, both of us. If you thought the water was poisoned, why—"

"—Not *that* water. The *bad* water. It's pretty, that water. Pretty to look at. Green. And it tastes nice. Like honey candy. It shines in the sun, too. But if you drink it, terrible things happen to you."

"How do you know this?"

"Well, everybody knows it. The people ... the people who had me, they showed it to me, that water. They told me how nice it would taste. Then they showed me a man. Like that tax man, only he was older. An old man. But he had the same head. All twisted. They said the old man used to drink that green water. When he was a boy. No one told him not to drink it, so he did. Then he couldn't stop drinking it. She was very nice, that time."

"Who was?"

"Gret. She didn't hurt me. She said they didn't want anything terrible to happen to me, I was too valuable. She told the others not to burn me. That's what they would do when they wanted to stop me from doing something, burn me. She told the others that I was used to the burning, so it wouldn't teach me anything. She said for them to take me to the man with the twisted head. *That* would stop me

from drinking the green water."

"Who is Gret?"

"The mother."

"Your mother?"

"No. I don't have a mother. I was saying the mother of Rem—the man with the jaw. And Lo, too. She's his sister."

"Gret was in charge?"

"I don't know what you mean."

"Gret was the one who told the others what to do?"

"Oh. Yes. Whatever she said, everyone had to do. That's why the others got killed, the little ones like me. They didn't always do what Gret said. That made them bad, when they did that. I *always* did what she said."

"If you always did what they said, why would they burn you?"

"I only would do what *Gret* told me. Rem was dumb. I could trick him, so he never burned me. But Lo would burn me for nothing. Just for ... I don't know why, I don't. But it wasn't for being bad, not like the others were."

"Did Lo hurt them, too?"

"Lo hurt everyone. Not Gret, nobody could do that. But everyone else, she hurt. I asked her why, once. That was the only time she burned me that I knew why she did it. She burned me for asking her a question. I never asked her anything after that."

"Your job was to tell men you had no one to play with?"

"Yes. I had to sit on the wall and put my knees together and my feet apart, then point my toes in. Lo showed me how."

"And get them to come back with you? Back into that portal?"

"That's right. They almost always did."

"Almost? Didn't they go back there most times?"

"Oh, no. Sometimes, a woman would tell me to come with her, but I was always too scared to do that. Lo would catch me—she's so very fast. And sometimes, a man would run. Run away, I mean. But, sometimes, when a man would stop and talk with me, he would look right past me. That's when he could see Lo. She would move around or something, I don't really understand it. But those men, they would just go by themselves. Lo was being bait ... that's the word Gret called her, bait."

"Those men, they would go to where they could see Lo?"

"I guess so. I wasn't supposed to look behind me. But I knew it would be the same thing as the men who came with me."

"Did they—the men, I mean—did *they* always come with you?"

"No, not them, either. And, some of them, I wasn't allowed to even ask."

"What kind of men?"

"If they had a dog with them, I couldn't be the bait. That was the rule."

"Do you know why?"

"No," the child said. "But it made me wish I had one. A dog, I mean."

Then she went so quiet that I felt it like a weight. One I had to carry. I didn't question that.

When we stopped, she sat next to me.

"What happened to the men who came with you?" I asked.

"Lo would hurt them. Rem would help her, sometimes. The things those men had, that's what we were supposed to get. That's what Gret told us."

"Things?"

"Whatever they had. It didn't matter. Tools. Food. Or even currency, sometimes. Then their clothing. 'Harvesting,' Gret said it was. Harvesting is when you dig a hole in the ground and put people in it. But, first, you take all their things. Everything they had. Then you put them in the ground."

"Who taught you that game?"

"How did you know that?"

"Know what?"

"That it *was* a game. That's what Gret said. She taught it to us. Lo could do it, too. She was the ... example! That's the word. I just remembered it. Gret said Lo would be the example. The example for me. Lo was too old to play the game like I did anymore, so she was the example. When I got old enough, then I would be the example."

"Was Lo the example for the other children, too?"

"Yes."

"The boys and the girl, all of them?"

"Oh, yes. Gret said boys are even better at it than girls. But only when they were little."

"Did they have names, those children?"

"I don't know."

"What were they called?"

"Oh. You mean like 'Stupid' Or 'Dirt'"

"Those aren't names."

"Yes, they are. I know they mean things, but they're names, too. 'Rem' and 'Lo'... those probably meant things, but I just don't know what."

"I know."

"You do? What did they—"

"—It doesn't matter."

"Because they're dead?"

"Because only people have names that matter. Those you call by name: Gret, Rem, Lo; they weren't people."

"I thought we were all... I mean.... Are you people?"

"Yes."

"I'm not, then, yes?"

"When you ask a question like that, how will you understand the answer? If I say 'Yes,' I am saying, 'Yes, you are not people.' And if I say 'No,' I am saying 'No, you are not people.' You see how that works?"

"I'm smart," she said, looking up at me almost as if she were testing defiance for the first time. "I don't tell people—I mean, I don't tell anyone, whoever they are. I have a lot of words. I can make words, too. Watch! 'I am not people.' Is that a true sentence?"

"No."

"Then I *am* people? People like you?"

"You're more kin to me than you were to Gret, Rem, and Lo."

"What is 'kin'"

"It comes from 'kinship.' That means, 'of the same blood.'"

"Blood is good?"

"Blood isn't good or bad. It just is."

"Gret and those others, they were all bad."

"All three of them, yes."

"No, all *six* of them. Just like Gret said."

"Gret said they were bad?"

"No. She didn't have to. Gret said bad people get themselves killed," the child said, as if reciting a mathematical formula. "When you don't act good, then you're bad. So, if you got yourself killed, then you must have been bad. The boys and the other girl, they got killed, so they were bad. When Gret and Rem and Lo got themselves killed, they were bad. Just like Gret always said: 'Bad gets killed.'"

I visually took the child's temperature, checking to see if emotion was going to overwhelm her. When I saw she wasn't going to break, I started walking again.

"What's there? On that tree? The one you're looking at so hard. Is it a message?"

"Those markings, the ones that look as if lightning struck through a stencil, those are runes."

"Wait! Stop. I don't know those words. That's not fair."

"It's not fair if I use words you don't know?"

"It's not! If I don't know what words mean, I could be bad and never know it. Then you'd kill me."

"Don't try to trick me," I said calmly. "That never works."

"You don't know—"

"—Yes, I do. You want me to tell you that you're not bad, so you'll be safe. But getting people to say words, that won't protect you."

I squatted in the grass, gesturing for the child to sit beside me. "If bad people get themselves killed, that's their fault, is that true?" I asked her.

"It *is* true. I told you—"

"—You told me what someone told *you*, nothing more. If bad people get *themselves* killed, that means their death was their own fault, right? So they couldn't know if they were bad *until* they got killed. That's what frightens you. The only weapons you have are your words, so you want to change *my* words."

"You're making my head hurt," the child said, her lower lip trembling in a practiced pout.

"Stop that. All those tricks they taught you, they're no good anymore. Don't do them again. Ever."

"What *am* I supposed to do, then?"

"You are supposed to listen. You are supposed to learn."

"If I do that, I won't be bad?"

"You won't be *acting* bad. You can't *be* bad, as if 'bad'

was a thing inside you, waiting to come out. People are bad when they do bad things. They don't *have* to do those things."

"Gret and Rem and Lo, they were bad. You said so. You said they weren't people."

"I also said you *were* people, didn't I?"

"Well.... Yes. But you killed them because they were bad, didn't you?"

"I killed them because they would have killed me."

"Not because they were bad?"

"Because they did bad *things*."

"Trying to kill you?"

"That was the *last* bad thing they did. But it wasn't the first. They made children do things. They hurt children. They used children to lure others. For the harvesting."

"All bad?"

"All bad," I confirmed.

"If people do enough bad, they're not people anymore?"

"That's the truth. A truth that says it all."

"So ... the other ones, the children I told you about, they were bad? Or no?"

"No."

"But you never met them. How could you say—"

"—Children can't be bad. They don't have the

possibility to make those kinds of choices. So they never resist things they are told to do. Some, some like you, they're very clever. They see they have to wait. That's what you were doing, isn't that true?"

"Waiting?"

"Yes."

"I ... guess I was. I don't know for what, exactly. But every day, when I sat at my post, I was waiting for someone to come along. The man who gave me my book, he wasn't afraid, like the others. I knew if I could wait long enough...."

"That was your job, waiting. But you weren't waiting for anyone to take you away."

"Maybe.... Maybe I was. But it didn't matter. I couldn't go with anyone, even if I wanted to. Gret and the others were always so close."

"And if you just ran, they'd catch you, right? So you were waiting for the right time to come."

"To run away?"

"I don't think so."

"What *do* you think?"

"You watched them. All of them. All the time," I said, seeing it all as I spoke. "You were waiting to kill them. A sharp stick, maybe. Or a heavy rock. Some of the people they harvested had things that made them all very sleepy.

You knew the sounds they made when they got sleepy from drinking some of the things they took from the people they harvested. Or maybe something they smoked. Or swallowed.

"You practiced pretending to be asleep. You watched to see how long they slept. How deep. Gret wouldn't share the things that made them sleepy, but, sometimes, there was so much of it that she fell asleep and there was still enough left for the others."

"How do you *know* this? I never told—"

"—But you had to be sure," I went on. "If you didn't kill them all...."

"That's right. Then it would be me who was bad."

"Because bad people get themselves killed?"

"I.... No! Because bad people kill you if you don't kill them. *That's* it, isn't it?"

"Yes. That's very good. The opposite of bad. Good. When you're searching for answers, true answers, you don't let anyone just tell you, you find out *for yourself.* Shortcuts look tempting, but they're always dangerous."

"Is that what we're doing? Searching for answers?"

"That's what you're doing. I have the answers I need. I'm looking for something else."

"What?"

"If you want *that* answer, you have to be very patient."

"Patient? Like waiting?"

"Yes. *Just* like that."

"Does that help you think?"

"This?" I asked her, holding up the yellow-paper cigarette.

"Yes. I didn't even see where you got it from."

I took another puff, not answering an unasked question.

"Will you tell me what that special writing means, now?"

"The ones on the tree?"

"Yes. With all the words."

I opened my codex. Showed her a page.

"I can see through the ... through the holes in the paper. You made ... you made a word!"

"Yes."

"It says 'Go.'"

"The paper is a stencil. When you spray something over a stencil, whatever is cut out of the stencil will be shown beneath it. Watch," I said. And showed her again.

"Yes," the child said, gravely. "So the lightning came through a stencil and left those marks on the tree?"

"That is what happened."

"But they're not words!"

"They're runes."

"Runes? You said that before. I don't have that word."

"It's from a language you don't know."

"But *you* know it."

"I don't know it. But I know how to ... translate it. That's why there's two stencils—one for the lightning, one for me."

"Well, what does it say, then?"

"It says we stand at the crossroads," I told her, repeating what I'd learned during my years of studying—all those years of waiting, never knowing for what, but focusing. Focusing on faith ... all I had. "Whenever a path forks, there is always guidance left behind by those who have gone before. Sometimes a ribbon, sometimes a bone. Other things, too. Those can be changed. But runes, those never change."

"I can *see* it. I mean, it's right in the middle. We could go straight. Or to the left, or the right."

"Or go back."

"But you're not going back."

"No."

"Then neither am I," she announced.

With the thumb and first two fingers of my right hand, I touched between my eyes, then tapped my heart, and,

finally, my left shoulder.

"That's only three."

"Yes?"

"Three places you touched. But the tree has four. Like ... branches, I mean."

"Not branches, choices."

"But there's *four* of them. And you only—"

"—For me, there are only three. Going back, that's not a choice."

"Why?"

"What I need to find, I know it's not behind me. So if I go back the way I've come, I'll *never* find it, see?"

"Why?"

"That's one of your good words, 'why.' But it's not a word you can use all the time."

"Wh...? I mean, how is that wrong?"

"It's not wrong. But that word—the word 'why'—it should be in your mind, not in your mouth. That way, you trust yourself, not what someone else tells you. Like that woman, Gret. Did you trust what she told you?"

"Yes."

"You trusted Gret?"

"I trusted her when she said thing-things."

"What's a thing-thing?"

"It's just a ... thing. Something you can see for yourself.

Or touch. Gret would say, if I did something wrong, I would get burned. And I always did. Get burned, I mean. So I trusted her when she said things like that. Thing-things. But I never trusted her when she said think-things."

I let my silence tell her I was listening.

"A think-thing is when you have to connect stuff. Like the other children—the older ones. When they were bad, they got killed. That's what Gret said, remember, I told you?"

"Yes."

"But I never *saw* them be bad, so I never knew why they got killed. Maybe it was what Gret said, but I never could be sure. So I was always...."

"Afraid?"

"I guess so. At first, anyway. But I knew they wouldn't kill me," the child said, with the calm assurance of an adult stating an accepted truth.

"How did you know this?"

"Because we all had jobs. The others, the children, they used to do the same job I did. But after they were killed, there was only me. Lo was too old, like I said. So they wouldn't kill me until they got another one. A younger one. Young is very important. But not too young—you have to be old enough to learn the game."

"So you trusted Gret not to kill you until they ... found another child?"

"Yes. But I knew they would. It was all in the days."

"The days?"

"The days," the child said, solemnly. "Days to get another one. One instead of me. If they got one that was too young, I would be safe until that one learned. That takes a lot of days. But I would never know how many. So I waited."

"To escape?"

"Maybe.... If I could really run away, I wouldn't have to get so far. Rem is very strong, but he isn't smart. Lo is fast, but she ... she doesn't pay attention, not for long. She could only do something for a little while, then she'd ... forget, like. And Gret, she never went much beyond the portal, even in the night. Never. No matter what."

"Where did you plan to go?"

"I don't know. I've never been to any other place."

"Didn't that frighten you?"

"Oh, no," the child said. "The worst that could be was already where I was."

I stood up. The child jumped lightly off the duffel where she had been perched. "So we go left?" she asked. "The last place you touched?"

"No. We go right. The direction I didn't touch."

"Is it far?" the child asked, an hour later.

"I don't know," I told her, truthfully.

"We just walk until we find it?"

"Or until we get tired. Or hungry. Then we rest. Or we eat. Or sleep."

"Until we find where you're traveling to?"

"Or until we find a place you want to stay. People you want to stay with."

"I want to stay with you."

"Why?"

"Hah! You used the word."

"I did," I acknowledged. "So what's the answer?"

"You won't hurt me."

"That's not enough."

"What else is there?"

"You'll see," I promised, internally questioning my own assurance—there was nothing in my own life to dispute the child's logic.

"You're taking me someplace!"

"No. I'm taking only myself."

"But I can come with you, isn't that true?"

"For now, it is."

"Be very quiet," I whispered, pulling the child gently by her wrist until she was crouched next to me.

"What are they?" she breathed.

"By the water hole? Those are traxxyls."

"I never saw anything like them. I don't have the word, either."

"Say what you see," I told her.

"I see.... They have thick plates on their bodies. And horns. They look like nothing could hurt them."

"People can hurt them," I told her, with the certainty of personal knowledge.

"Why would people want to hurt them?"

"For their horns."

"I don't understand."

"People kill them. To harvest their horns."

"Harvest? They kill them? And cut off their horns?"

"Yes. They grind the horns into powder. Then they trade the powder for things they want."

"Oh. I.... Wait! The powder, do people keep it in what they call 'tins?' Little metal things, with tops that come off?"

"Sometimes, yes."

"I saw Gret take one of those, once. She said, 'Bring me

the green tin,' to Lo. When she turned the top, there was this white powder inside. She said the powder was currency."

"For some, it is."

"How do people kill the ... traxxyls, right?"

"Yes, traxxyls. They kill them many different ways."

"Are people going to come and kill those over there?"

"People are killing them right now."

"I don't see any—"

"—The water hole," I explained. "It's poisoned. The killers put the poison in there, so they can kill entire herds at the same time. Kill from a distance, keeping themselves safe from those same horns they want to harvest."

"But don't those traxxyls know the water is bad?"

"No, they don't. It's like that green water you told me about."

"So they're all going to die? Every one of them?"

"Yes."

"I don't want them to die!" the child said, fervently.

"It is too late," I told her. Again, truthfully.

The child tugged my sleeve urgently. "Not for the rest of them. *See!* The ones waiting to drink. They're not poisoned yet, are they?"

"No. Not yet. But—"

She suddenly sprang to her feet, waving her arms

frantically, screaming: "Run away! Run away!"

The herd of traxxyls turned as one, their enormous eyes swiveling to take in the source of the noise. They stood stolidly, slowly computing.

"Make them run!" the child demanded.

I reached into the duffel, took out a stoppered glass vial, pulled the cork, and sprinkled a few grains of a red substance into my palm. "Blow across this," I told her. "Toward where the traxxyls are."

She filled her lungs and sharply expelled a breath.

The red grains became a small cloud. As the cloud moved toward the herd of traxxyls, it crackled and sparked, powered by the child's heart.

The traxxyls bolted.

"Come back into the brush," I whispered. "We don't know what will happen next."

"Will they be safe now?" the child asked, later. "The traxxyls?"

"The ones who didn't drink, yes."

"The ones who did, they'll all die?"

"Yes."

"And be harvested?"

"Yes."

"What happens then?"

"Like I told you, the harvesters will sell the powder they make."

"That's not—"

"—And those who use that powder will die."

"Why? Uh ... I mean, how come?"

"The horns of the traxxyls are actually hair," I told her. "Hair that grows from their heads. The hair hardens until it forms into the horns. Whatever goes into their bodies is drawn into the hair. The poison that kills the traxxyls works very slowly. By the time they die, it will have traveled all the way into their horns."

"So when the harvesters grind up the horns, they're really making poison?"

"Yes."

"Good!"

"It is good," I agreed. "And fair enough. The people who consume the powder believe it helps them ... do things. That's a very old belief. Been around for years. Many, *many* years. It will take as long again for beliefs like that to die. And—"

"—Wait! What things? What things will it help them do?"

"Things they want to do. Things they believe they need to do to keep themselves ... powerful."

"Oh."

"Those things are very important to such people," I said, trying to explain what I knew for truth, while skirting its ugliness. "So they will pay almost anything for that powder. And that makes the powder valuable. That's why some others kill the traxxyls, to *make* that powder."

"Currency," the child said, solemnly.

"That's right. Currency."

"But if the powder is poison...?"

"I know that. Now, *you* know that, too. But the people who want the power, *they* don't know. They don't know the powder is poison any more than the traxxyls knew the water was. It will take many lifetimes before everybody knows. When everybody *believes.* Only when enough people die from the powder will it stop being worth anything. Then, no more harvesting of traxxyls."

"So ... many, *many* years?"

"Yes."

"I wish it could be right now."

"Wishes don't change things. But what you wish for this time, that will happen."

"But not now. What happens *now?*"

"That water hole, the traxxyls won't come back to it."

"But won't the bad people just poison a different one?"

I didn't have an answer for her, so I started walking again.

"The people who harvest the traxxyls?"

"What?" I said, knowing more was coming.

"Those people put poison in the water. And that same poison, it will make people stop the harvesting?"

"Eventually."

"So they're really killing the killers?"

"Very good," I told her, not sarcastically.

"It *is* very good. But it will take such a long time. Is that how it always has to happen?"

"Most change—*lasting* change—that takes a very long time, true enough."

"So we won't see it?"

"Not with our eyes. Not to touch."

"So how do you know? How do you know for sure?"

"Sometimes, when you see the beginning clearly enough, you can see the end."

"I don't have the words for that."

"You don't need words for everything."

"What else could I—"

"—You have your senses," I told her, thinking of all my time in solitary. "Your eyes, your ears, your nose. Your touch. And your tongue."

"Is that all?"

"Is that all for you? I don't know."

"You!" the child almost shouted. Then snapped her mouth closed as if to prevent something of great value from escaping.

A kilometer or so in silence, then: "How do you know things?"

"Know what things?" I asked the child.

"Things, like ... traxxyls, you called those ... animals. I know 'animals.' I have that word. But not 'traxxyl.'"

"Your word-book doesn't have all the words. And it doesn't have pictures, so—"

"—Pictures?! There's a word-book with pictures?"

"Some pictures. A word-book with pictures, that

would be an encyclopedia."

"Encyclopedia," she repeated to herself, as if committing the word to memory. "Do you have one?"

"No, I don't."

"Could we *get* one?"

"I don't know. They're pretty old books. Where I come from, people use library screens when they want to see pictures of words."

"What's a—"

"They don't have them here."

"Here?"

"Where we are. 'Here' is where we are."

"But you're here, too. Like me."

"I am now. But I came from another place."

"There's—"

"Yes. There's another place," I told her, hoping for a way to have that talk later. I didn't know when later would be. Or if it ever would.

And then the butterfly landed and everything changed. It was very large. Two of its four wings were white with black stripes, the other two were black with white stripes, as if two halves had been welded together to the sides of the body, which was a brilliant electric blue. I'd never seen one like it in real life, but I had on the library screen. I didn't know its name, but I recognized it for what it was.

So I was ready when....

"What is—"

"—It's a gynandro," I told her. "I know you don't have the word. That isn't the name of that butterfly; I don't *know* its name. A gynandro is a *kind* of creature."

"Not just butterflies?"

"Not just butterflies. It means a creature that is half male, half female."

"A boy *and* a girl? At the same time?"

"Yes."

"How does that happen?"

"It's an accident. An accident of nature."

"So they can't have more?"

"Why would you say that?"

"Well, if it's an accident, that just ... happens, doesn't it? I mean, a black cat and a white cat could have all different colored kittens, but...."

"That's true," I told her, impressed again. "If you had two butterflies like that one, and they ... mated, they wouldn't be making more of their own kind."

"I wonder if they're sad," she said. "If I was them, I would be."

If the pace tired the child, she gave no sign.

"What are those?" she asked, frantically stabbing her forefinger into the air before her eyes."

"Those? Use your words. You could mean—"

"—Those little ... they're moving too fast for me to point at them. Like ... little jewels. *See?*"

I did see. "Hummingbirds," I told her.

"They're not humming."

"Not a hum with the mouth, they hum when they disturb the air with their speed."

"They're so pretty. Why don't they ... land, or something?"

"They're trap-lining."

"I don't know that word," the child said, her voice heavy with the patience of an elder addressing a youth.

"Trap-lining is how you locate what you marked before. So you can return to those places. Like a map," I explained, thinking how everything in my life always circled back to the same path.

"Where do they want to go?"

"To fuchsia. A tiny little flower. It looks like a bell in two shades of purple. The dark purple on the inside holds nectar. That's their food."

"Can we find some?"

"If we walk the same path as the hummingbirds."

"Couldn't we do that?"

"We could. But I'm not—"

"—Please!"

"Ssssh! Shouting is a mistake."

"Okay. But *can* we?"

"Maybe."

"Isn't that up to you?"

"It is up to the path," I told her. Meaning, I was going to walk my path. If there were hummingbirds along it, then....

"I want to see the birds!"

"I told you how you could do that."

"But they're *gone*. And I don't know which way they went."

"Neither do I. But I know where I have to go. If the birds find their nectar along that path, I'll see them."

"What about me?"

"You have a choice."

"Like before?"

"Like always," I said.

"*Oh!*"

The child stood, transfixed, watching an endless array of tiny flicks of darting color, glittering in the sunlight.

I kept walking.

"Wait!" she hissed. "You'll scare them."

"No, we won't," I said. "Hummingbirds are fearless. Look. See those cats?"

"I don't... Yes! There they are. *Big* ones, too."

"Cats will kill birds, right?"

"They will! Once I saw—"

"—They'll kill birds if they can. Wounded birds. Sometimes, birds in nests. But they can't kill *those* birds."

"Because they're too fast?"

"Much too fast. If you're patient, if you stay *still*, you can watch a single fuchsia bell. Narrow your eyes and concentrate on it. Sooner or later, one of the birds will come to feed. If you stand *still*, you'll see another reason why these birds don't fear the cats."

"I can be quiet for a long time."

"I know."

"How do you—"

"—Ssssh."

"There's one. He's so ... he's just ... floating there. Where are his wings? How does he—"

"—Those birds have wings. But they move them so fast your eyes can't see anything but a blur. Look closely..."

"I see them! I see the wings!"

"Good. Now look at how the bird feeds."

"His ... beak? It's so *long.* Is that what you meant?"

"Yes. That beak is very strong. And that bird is very fast. Like this," I said softly, flicking my suddenly-opened hand.

A metal spike appeared in the trunk of a nearby tree.

"Did you...? I mean... How did you do that?"

Instead of answering, I stepped to the tree, braced my right palm against the trunk and pulled the spike out with my left. Kneeling, I showed it to the child. "You see? The tip of this is tiny, like the beak of the hummingbird. And sharp, too. When a tiny, pointed thing moves *very* fast, it can penetrate anything."

"Like a bullet?"

"What do you know about bullets?" I asked, masking my surprise.

"A bullet comes from a gun."

"All right, then. What do you know about guns?"

"A gun shoots bullets."

"Have you ever seen a gun?" I asked, patiently.

"No. But I have the word, so it's mine. To know, I mean."

"This is a spike, not a bullet."

"I know that, too. But when you ... when you made it fly, it was like *you* were a gun."

"Huh! Good enough. So, now do you understand why the birds don't fear those cats?"

"Yes. Because they have spikes, too. Only their spikes don't ... jump, like yours did. They're ... attached. They're part of that bird, that means. So if they were going fast enough, and they hit one of those cats...."

"Right. And the birds know that. Just like the cats know it. So those birds and the cats, they can be very close to each other without danger to either."

"But what is there for the cats to eat?"

"Look down the road. Past the fuchsia. What do you see?"

"That's ... that's metal."

"A building. Once people lived there. Whatever lives there now is food for the cats. For those cats quick enough, anyway. Come on."

"Why are we going there?"

"There?"

"To that building. What you called a building, anyway. I have that word, but that ... that doesn't look like my word."

"It is what remains of your word. Do you have 'city'?"

"Yes. There would be a lot of buildings. Real buildings,

not just that mess of rusty metal."

"The rusted metal is what's left of a building. The building was once part of a city."

"What happened to it?"

"It died," I told her.

"Like when things get very old? Or did something kill it?"

"Why would that matter?"

"Because 'dead is dead,' you mean? Gret used to say that all the time."

"When would Gret say that?"

"Whenever Lo got travelers to come in so she and Rem could make them die. Gret said people die when they get too old to find food. Or too old to eat what got found for them. And that's the same 'dead' as what Lo and Rem would do to them. That's what she said. It didn't matter how it happened or when it happened; it was all the same."

Each step brought us closer to the I-beamed skeleton. Sun glinted through the clearing, bouncing in near-blinding intensity off rolls of tin sheeting that formed several connected roof structures.

"Stay behind me," I told her.

"Why?"

I held out my open palm. The child reacted instantly, merging herself into my shadow as though she had been

trained to the signal.

The forest sounded a soft death rattle, then went silent.

As we closed on the interlocking structures, the darkness re-formed itself into a maze of corridors. I knew what spell-word to use. My hands were empty, but I walked through the corridor walls as if they were dry straw and I was holding a flamethrower.

The child followed silently in my wake.

"Stop there!" a voice came from a pool of black.

I did, trusting the child would do the same.

"You know the tricks of light, do you?" the voice came again.

"Some of them," I answered.

"Only I speak, but there are many of us."

I shrugged one shoulder, allowing my duffel to fall to the ground. I took another step forward, clasping my left wrist in my right hand.

"And we are only two," I said.

"You are wise to disclose," the voice came. "We saw the small one behind you as you approached. Why conceal?"

"Not conceal. Protect."

"Is that a child, then?"

"Yes."

"Your child?"

"Ask a different question," I said, calming my center,

getting ready.

"You, a stranger, you command us?"

"I only advise you," I said.

Silence descended.

"You are a patient man."

I didn't answer. And wasn't surprised that the child's stillness had matched mine.

"What do you seek here?"

"A cartographer," I told him, lying with the truth. The mapmaker hadn't been a blooded-in Dark White member. He had his ink, but he hadn't earned it yet, so he hadn't been full-trusted. Whatever the leader code-talked, he drew. It was set up so that the cartographer couldn't read his own map. All he'd know is the last place the map had been. I'd be able to read it if I could just look at it once, but now only the cartographer knew where it was. What I didn't know was where *he* was. I hadn't found him in the Sector. He could be here, hiding in the Pure Zone, all his markings intact.

Or as dead as my chances.

The cops had cut me free to find a killer. A contract. One I was still working—there was no time limit. I could find him eventually; I was sure of that. And equally sure I

wouldn't be returning to prison. But still not truly free—finding the map was the only way to become that.

But what I was doing for the Synthetic Woman, what had brought me to this place, that had to be done first. Because even if I found the cartographer, I might still need her to get me to the marked spot.

I'd rolled every set of cubes I could find, but hadn't hit the combination. Only the Synthetic Woman was a sure bet. So I was standing in darkness, waiting for the next question, prepared to lie or tell the truth, depending on need.

"By what name is this cartographer known?" the voice demanded.

"He has no name you would know."

"Say his name, *then* we will know."

"There is no need," I told him. "I will look with my eyes, not with your ears."

"You expect to enter without permission?"

"I would prefer your permission," I said gently, the implication left unsaid.

Silence dropped its curtain again.

"Do you know what is three and four?" the voice came.

"Seven!" the child burst out.

"Seven is correct," the voice said. "That is a number of magick. Do you know it?"

"I know what I know," I answered. Quickly, before the child could jump in again.

"Everyone knows what they know," the voice said.

"No, they don't," I told him, truthfully.

"Ah!" the voice said, as if addressing an audience. "The stranger speaks in tongues."

I held up my right hand, palm toward the voice. A gasp came from the child, vibrating through the darkness and bouncing back. My extended hand was five fingers, bracketed by a thumb on each side.

"Seven," the child whispered.

Again, the word reverberated out and returned.

"Our game is named for magick," the voice said. "Three-Four/Four-Three it is called. If you agree to play, you may enter. If you win, you may search with your eyes. You agree that is fair?"

"Yes."

"This too is fair: if you lose, you leave."

"Understood."

"But then you leave alone. The little one stays with us."

"Bargain!" the child yelled.

"You speak for the stranger?" the voice asked her.

"Just for me," the child said. "But it doesn't matter; he won't lose."

"Your father cannot know our game."

"He isn't my father. And it *still* doesn't matter."

"You agree?" the voice asked.

"Yes," I said. Robbed of choices. Again.

The light shifted again, revealing descending steps.

"Slowly," I cautioned the child.

Thirteen steps brought us to a rectangular room, lined by tiers of murk on all sides. In the center of the room was a green felt billiard table, its dimensions a precise percentage of the surrounding walls. Sixteen balls were racked in a diamond shape:

8

14 2

5 7 6

1 4 12 13

10 9 11

15 3

88

"We do not acknowledge pure white," the voice said, as a zebra-striped ball appeared at the end of the table opposite the rack. "Pure white is the absence of all color, as pure black is the presence of all. What we cannot see with our eyes. What the sky-watchers call "dark matter." So. Have you played three-four/four-three before?"

"No," I told the voice.

"Then we will explain. Only these numbers matter: two and three, fourteen and fifteen. You see the ball marked eight-eight? The one that keeps changing color? If it should be pocketed before its time, the shooter loses. Do you understand?"

"Yes."

"The balls must be struck in numerical order, starting with Number One. There is a pocket in each corner, and one in the center of each longitudinal rail. They will open as a ball approaches, and close around any ball accurately placed within their center."

The voice paused as if expecting questions. When I stayed silent, it continued:

"The value of each ball is in its number. So you are wondering, what if one player should pocket the Three and the Fourteen while the other the Two and the Fifteen, yes? That would be a tie, and another game would be required, you might think. But that is where the eight-

eight is allowed. In the event of a tie, whoever pockets that ball is the winner. Is that clear?"

"It is."

"You have not played before?"

"I said that."

"You did. Very well. Would you like to go first?"

"It doesn't matter."

"Ah, you tell the truth with that."

A faint vibration came from the tiered murkiness as a tiny man stepped forward, carrying a cue of dark red wood banded in yellow and black. A small stepladder rolled to his side.

I could feel the child vibrate with wonderment as this perfect replica of a full-grown man moved into the light, but I'd seen plenty of his kind before. They hold an entire area of the Sector to themselves—hire themselves out to do deep-tunnel work.

The homunculus climbed the stepladder, draped his left forearm over the top step, elevated his right elbow, and stroked the zebra-striped ball smoothly. The ball traveled parallel to the left side of the rack, then suddenly hooked to squarely strike the One, scattering the colored balls.

The Two entered the right top corner pocket, the Three the lower right. The Fourteen dropped into the

opened upper left as the Four rolled toward the lower right.

And stopped.

The zebra-striped ball was behind a wall of color.

The homunc never changed expression as he slapped his palm against the top step of the ladder, causing it to roll to a stop behind the zebra-striped ball. Again, he elevated his elbow and stroked.

The zebra-striped ball looped around the clot of accumulated colors, darting toward the One as if guided by a laser.

And stopped.

"You are a cheat," the voice said.

"It is your table," I answered him. "And your rules."

"Sorcery is not allowed to enter this place."

"It is your table," I repeated. "And your rules. You invited me in."

"Yes. And, now, you are barred."

"It is too late for that, now. You allowed me to enter, so your screens didn't detect sorcery. That makes *you* the cheater."

"You confuse skill with—"

"—I am not confused," I interrupted, keeping my voice measured, preparing to formal-speak. "It is your champion who has no skill. And you have no honor. Your

champion is a wizard, yet you claim to bar sorcery from entering his arena. Your arena."

"We all saw the strike-ball stop," the voice said. "That is within the nature of the object. Only sorcery could make that happen."

"Sorcery? Because a ball stopped?" I said, addressing an audience I couldn't see. "But *not* because a ball curved? You yourself said your game is named for magick."

The voice laughed, a sound like delicate glass dropped from a great height onto a bed of heavy sand. "Magick is barred from *entering*. Do you understand *now*?"

"Yes, I understand," I said, struggling to stay formal. "What you call a 'game' is not a contest. You practice magick, but you bar magick from your presence. By your practices, you are known. So you are a cheat."

"Me?"

"All of you."

"You cannot judge us."

"Are you so certain? As certain as you were that magick cannot enter your house?"

"You will go now. And leave the child."

She instantly ducked behind me, as if to make herself invisible.

"Yes, we'll go now. I have the stake I played for."

"You played for no—"

"—I played. I played fairly. And I know the cartographer isn't here."

"How could you know that? No permission was granted for you to search. You did not win. The game cannot be won without sorcery, and sorcery is not allowed."

"*Incoming* sorcery."

"If you say."

"I say."

"You cannot say our rules."

"Those rules have changed," I told him, letting an organ-stop of force into my voice. "If you stand aside, we will go. If you do not, the game continues. But, if the game continues, the stakes have changed, too."

"You threaten us?"

"No," I said, pointing my cue stick like a wand at the table. The zebra-striped ball jumped two inches off the felt, dropped back, and began to rotate in place. Then it slowly rolled toward the One Ball, tapped it gently, and reversed itself, moving the length of the table until it dropped the Fifteen ball, leaving the ball marked Eight-Eight exposed right behind the One.

"What happens next is your decision," I told the unseen audience.

The poolroom dropped into a thick, dense silence.

Time passed.

"Go!" the voice said, pretending that was a command.

"Were those bad people?" the child asked as the city of ruined people disappeared behind us.

"Was Gret bad?" I challenged her.

"I ... I don't have that word the same. Not anymore."

"What do you have now?"

"I have.... I have 'good.' That word is an antonym. An antonym for 'bad.' An antonym means the opposite. Like 'up' and 'down.' So maybe I don't know what 'bad' is, not exactly. But I know it's not good. Is that the truth?"

"It is true for you."

"What does that mean? Isn't a thing true for everyone?"

"No." I sat down, took a dark yellow cigarette from my jacket.

"Can I have one, too?"

"You are not grown enough."

"Why?"

"Didn't I tell you—"

"—I know. I know. I'm sorry. But you have to tell me, don't you? I'm old enough for what you eat, aren't I? I mean, you let me share and—"

"—Yes, you are grown enough to eat what I eat."

"And drink what you drink?"

"That, too."

"So why am I not grown enough for your cigarette?" she demanded.

"Because my cigarette doesn't work the same on children," I told her.

"We're not all alike."

"Who?"

"Children. We're different. Remember I told you about—"

"—Yes, I remember. But no child would be able to taste my cigarette."

"That's not fair."

"Many things aren't fair. They just are."

"Like what?"

"Rain."

"What?"

"Rain falls on everyone. Some have shelter, some don't. Rain doesn't make decisions; it just falls."

"I want to try," the child insisted.

I shrugged a "too bad." She just sat there, watching me. After a long moment, I handed the cigarette over.

The child placed the yellow leaf between her lips. "I know how to do this. I saw people do it. Plenty of times.

Just watch."

She inhaled deeply. Her chest swelled. Her eyes narrowed.

"It isn't lit!"

I took the cigarette from her hands, put it to my mouth and inhaled. Smoke slowly bubbled out my nostrils. I inhaled again and blew a stream of smoke over the child's head. Then I handed her the cigarette.

She tried again.

"It doesn't work!"

"It doesn't work for you."

"That's not...."

I took the cigarette back from her.

The child was content to sit beside me in silence, perhaps sensing that the next direction was not known to me. By then, I knew: To find the cartographer, I'd have to travel within myself.

I heard them approach, but gave no sign.

Two of them. Not young men, but not far past that time in their lives. Despite the belongings-carriers slung over their shoulders, they weren't travelers. Whatever their purpose, they moved with the precision of a team, one with many hours invested in practice.

I kept my hands visible, listening to the child's quickened heartbeat.

The two men stayed within arm's length of each other, signaling they were peaceable. They made no attempt to separate, not forcing me to choose between them for defense.

"Night will come soon," the taller one said. "Do you have shelter?"

All travelers know that question. If they answer "No," they will be offered a place to sleep, perhaps even some food. If they answer "Yes," they will be asked to share.

"Are you concerned for our safety?" I asked.

They looked at each other. Meaningfully, but still without menace.

"A man can never have too many friends," the taller one said.

I didn't answer. Instead, I pulled my cigarette from the blossoming pocket, took a deep drag, then handed it to the child.

"You don't offer to share tobacco?" the shorter one said. His voice was harsher than his partner's, suiting his role in their team.

I didn't answer. I accepted the cigarette back from the child, proud of her calmness.

"Is she yours?" the taller one said.

I knew what that question meant on this side of the Kangol. Now all that remained was to play the script. I was on my feet before either of them could react.

"This spot is not ours," I told them. "We don't claim it. We will leave it to you."

"You didn't answer the question," the shorter one said.

"I am not a merchant," I replied.

"Here, everyone's a merchant," the taller one said, his voice slick with the oil of certainty. "Everyone buys or sells. Or trades. Outside the towns, even the growers have to trade. We carry currency. You know how important that is. Will you answer our question now?"

"I have answered your question," I said. As the taller one's left hand flicked out toward my face, I stepped to my right, snatching his wrist with my own left hand. I pulled him close as my right hand came across—the first two knuckles cracked against his temple.

His partner was quick, but their rehearsals hadn't covered the problem of a body between him and his target. I pointed my toe skyward and shoved with my heel, rolling the body of the taller man into the knees of the shorter one, bending him at the waist. The edge of my hand found the vertebrae at the back of his neck and it was over.

"Are they dead?" the child said.

"Not yet."

"Will they die?"

"Soon."

"From what you did?"

"From what *they* did."

"You mean, if they hadn't—"

"—Yes. But their death will come at the hands of others. The things inside their belonging-carriers will bring scavengers out."

"Do you have a knife?"

"Why do you ask?"

"We should kill them," she said, solemnly.

"Why...." I started to ask, then checked myself, "They're no threat to us now."

"But they're *dying*," the child said. "That must hurt. We could stop them from hurting if we had a knife."

"Did you ever stop anyone from hurting?" I asked her.

"Not a ... not a person. A cat. A little cat. I found it. Out by my wall. Someone had thrown it against the stone. It was all bloody. And crying. I could tell it was hurt. Very bad hurt. I didn't want it to hurt. And I couldn't make it better. I had a little knife. Not really a knife, just a piece of the blade. It wasn't sharp, but it had a point. I ... pushed it into the little cat. Hard. And then she stopped crying."

"That's why you're crying now?"

"I am not!" she said vehemently, refusing to move.

I didn't need any of my knives to do what she wanted.

In the days that followed, we passed many others. Some coming toward us, moving in our opposite direction; others we passed because they were moving slowly, encumbered by possessions or infirmities.

All were either seekers or drifters. No travelers, so greetings were rare, questions never asked. Some offered to trade, none offered to share.

The only thing of importance: none threatened.

We never moved in darkness. This far past the Kangol, there were no agreed-upon signals for peacefulness ... and even if such had existed, none would have been trusted.

"What is that stuff?" the child asked the first night.

"Seismic Dust," I told her, sprinkling more of the powder around the perimeter I had established, thinking of a living shadow people called Sonar. "It detects waves of sound."

"Like those night birds?"

"No. The birds all make sounds of their own. Sounds we can hear."

"But those birds hear, too, don't they? Isn't that how they hunt?"

"They hunt with their eyes."

"They can see in the dark?"

"To them, it's no great trick. Their eyes can pull light from dark."

"That's why they don't come out in the daytime? Because the light would hurt their eyes?"

"Yes."

"But why—I mean, *how*, how can that powder see? It doesn't have any eyes."

I plucked a hollow reed from a marsh bed, and held it to the child's ear.

"I can't hear anything."

I tapped the reed several times with my fingernail.

"Oh!"

"Those are vibrations. Do you have the word?"

"Yes! When something moves back-and-forth, it vibrates. Like the hummingbirds? Their wings?"

"That's right. When something vibrates, it disturbs the air. Anything that disturbs the air makes sounds. Some we can hear, some we can't," I said, as I placed a dry twig on the ground. "Step on that." I told her.

The *snap!* was as sharp as a pistol shot.

"When you step on the ground, the ground vibrates, but you don't hear it because the sounds it makes are too soft. This powder makes the ground under it be like that dry twig. If anyone steps on it, I'll hear it."

"So inside the circle you're making ... with that powder, I mean ... inside that, we're safe?"

"Yes."

The child curled up and instantly fell asleep.

Every day, we walked. Each night, we camped, always within the perimeter we created.

"Do you know where we're going?" she asked one morning.

"Not specifically."

"I don't have that word."

"I don't know an exact place. Not yet."

"But...."

"Here's how it works: What I'm looking for, it hasn't been in any place I've looked. So it has to be in a place I *haven't* looked, understand?"

"Sure! Like if you lost something. You look in one place, and if it's not there, you look in another place."

I just nodded, thinking the child's patience wasn't inborn. I knew patience was a skill acquired by practice. And that a true commitment is necessary—to learn patience, one must *be* patient. The child's patience had come to her at high speed due to the narrowness of her choices. The Venturi effect, I remember reading ... physics

and kinetics. Destination had no meaning for the child. For her, distance was everything.

The three women flowed naturally into a self-defense fan, allowing us room to pass.

"Hello!" the child called out.

The shortest of the three stepped slightly forward, her eyes never leaving mine.

"Is the child yours?"

"Why do you ask?" I answered.

"If she is not, perhaps she would like to come with us," the woman said, shifting the walking stick she carried to her off-hand.

"No, thank you," the child said, very politely.

"You are not a trader?" she asked me.

"I trade my work for whatever I need."

"Only your work?"

"Only my work."

The woman on her right stepped closer. "Do you take contracts?"

"I take *some* contracts," I said, carefully.

"Will you let us read the cards first?" the third one said.

We sat down at the side of the road, arranging ourselves so we could watch all those who passed.

The women spread a blanket the same color as the ground. The third one took an ebony box from her pack. Looking steadily at me, she shook it briskly and flicked her wrist. A card emerged.

"There's nothing on it," the child said, clearly disappointed.

The woman repeated the gesture. Another card fell.

"It's the same," the child said, as if cheated out of something she had been promised.

Five more gestures. Seven blank cards on the blanket.

The second woman forked her fingers, aimed them at her eyes, then pointed the same two fingers at the child. Then she turned the cards over. Deliberately, one by one.

Fire.

Lightning.

Rain.

Fog.

Snow.

Sun.

An arrow embedded in a boulder.

"Oh!" the child exclaimed.

The reader extended her hands, one to the dealer, one to the leader.

They went into their own silence.

The child waited with me. Patiently.

"Cards are truth," the leader finally said. "There are many ways to work with cards, but the cards themselves do not change."

I gave her silence. So did the child. I was proud of her.

"In the Sector, there is a game. A game with cards. It is called 'bridge.' In this, in the Pure Zone, the bridge is our destination."

"The Kangol?" the child blurted out. I didn't try to guess where she had come by the name ... a traveler, perhaps? One who could point the way, but wouldn't walk it himself.

"Yes," the woman said. "That is the path to where we must go. But we cannot cross until we have our Fourth."

"One more of you?"

"Yes."

I stayed silent.

"That's the contract!" the child said, excitedly. "That's the contract, isn't it? You want us to find your ... Fourth, right?"

All three women bowed slightly, as if in deference to the child's understanding.

"We can do it," the child said.

"No promises," I said, careful not to contradict her, but mindful of realities. "And you haven't heard the bargain yet."

"Say the bargain," the dealer spoke.

"You know how to cross," I said, shifting position just enough to be sure all three knew I was including them, watching their eyes to see if the words I'd just spoken reflected as their truth. "There is no doubt in you, so you've already made the deal. I don't know how you summon a Cargo Car, and I accept that this is not *for* me to know. But this I will know now, or we have no contract. You said you could not go with less than four, yes? Could it be more?"

"It is not a great distance," the reader said.

"Not in kilometers," I answered. "But the transporters don't charge by such a measure."

"So?"

"So, did you buy the car, or just a share?"

"The car," the dealer said. "The entire car."

"Done, then," I told them, bowing just enough to keep them all within my sight. "How will I know your Fourth?"

"Watch our eyes," the leader said.

I scanned. They didn't look alike, much less like sisters, but their eyes were all the same color as their blanket, as if

interchangeable between them. Again, they touched hands. As they did, their eyes glowed, color-shifting to a golden bronze, then to a dark garnet, then back to their first color.

"Our Fourth has the same eyes," the leader said. "Only the eyes. The rest of her will appear to you as pure-pure."

"What?"

"The cards say your markings are a disguise," she said. "So let us see."

I said nothing, waiting for whatever was to come.

"There is a word that will snap any lock," she said. "It can be called, but never *recalled*. Do you ken?"

"A word that kills synthetics?"

"Aye," the leader said. "And our cards tell us you are one of those."

"A synthetic? Not in this zone, I'm not."

"Your markings traveled with you."

"Markings on my skin, only."

"So you tell us. Still, you know why others call this zone 'pure?'"

"I do."

"Then you know that term has a different meaning for each who speaks it?"

"That, too."

"Then you *already* know the word."

"If so?" I said, giving them nothing.

"If so, our Fourth will appear to you as she appears to those of your kind. Of the kind you guise yourself as."

I clasped my hands at my waist, telling her she hadn't told me enough. Although she truly had.

"You know the word to say to those who have our Fourth?"

"I do, now."

"If you lie, you—"

"—die, yes. So you say. But the word, the word itself has no universal meaning—it does not carry its own purity. For some, it matches my ink. But the ink is mine, so I know its truth. And I say it does not match."

"When you accepted your ink, you believed in that purity?"

"My ink wasn't accepted, it was sought. But what I sought was not purity, it was freedom. Whatever that cost, freedom."

"Whatever that cost you?"

"Or anyone else."

"Come back tomorrow," the leader said.

"Don't be mad," the child said, tugging at the strap of my duffel as we walked off.

"Why would I—"

"—You said it first!" she half-shouted. "'Why.' You said it. So when I—"

"—Ask your question," I told her, impressed with her manipulation skills even as I realized I'd lost more than the one round. Going forward, that "Why?" gateway would be forever open.

"Why did they tell us to come back? Why didn't they just make the contract?"

"Because I told them I am not a trustworthy man."

"But you *are!*" I have that word. I know what it means. You do what you say you're going to do. They don't know you."

"I'm the one who told them."

"But they don't *know* you."

"And you do?"

"Yes," she said, all the child gone from her voice.

"Let us have our food," is all I said.

"You have these words?" I asked her, later. "Past, present, future?"

"I have the words. But I don't have the—I don't have the ... feelings, maybe?"

"The past was yesterday. The present is right now. The

future is tomorrow."

"But.... There were days before yesterday. And there will be days after...."

"Yes. That's what I was telling those women. Today, I told them that I was untrustworthy. I *was* untrustworthy ... I was *once* untrustworthy, do you see? Then, my word could be trusted, but not me. I, myself, I could not be trusted. That was when I was what they called me ... a synthetic. I tell them that truth about the past—now, in the present, I tell them—so they can trust me in the future."

"Oh. Does that work?"

"Tomorrow, we'll know."

"Your past is dark," the leader said the next day.

"So might be my future," I agreed.

"You came here seeking.... What?"

"It doesn't matter what it's called. Money, gold, currency."

"You are from the Sector. Paper is of no value there. Only the ore."

"I know. I'm not looking for money, not here. Here, I'm looking for a map."

"The map is here?"

"No."

"So you seek the cartographer?"

"As I told you from the beginning."

"But that was a lie."

"No. Not a lie. I know the Faiths don't use treasure maps."

"Ah. So you know of us. Then you seek a map to ... what?"

"To what I seek," I answered. Not a riddle, saying that I was done saying. "My words, for my word: I want a cartographer, yes. But not a cartographer *with* a map, a cartographer to *draw* a map."

"A map to a map, then?"

"Yes."

"Will you sit for another reading?"

"I will."

"And the child...?"

"The child stays with me. Understand?"

The three Faiths exchanged nods.

"Are we agreed, then? Our Fourth for a meeting with the cartographer."

"And the words."

"Words? We told you there would be *a* word ... a word

you already know. The risk-to-you word."

"The word to snap the lock, that I have. But, also, the word to summon the transporter. And the word to open the bin of the Cargo Car you bought."

"Yes. We will honor that."

"And one more."

"To do what?"

"To summon-and-release."

"One word for all that?"

"For all that and more."

"We do not trade in words-without-limit."

"I want no such word."

"Then tell us."

"You mean, 'trust us.'"

"As we would be trusting you."

"Stay still," I told the child. Then I stepped close to the Faiths, and told them the truth.

"Weren't we supposed to get something, too?" the child asked that night.

"What should we have gotten?"

"I don't know. But ... *something*, shouldn't we? A contract, that's when you do something and you get something. It's a ... transaction, isn't it? You give

somebody what they want, and they give you what you want."

"True."

"Well, what do *we* want?"

"They already know," I told her. "That was in their cards, too."

"But *I* don't know," she said, indignantly. "All that stuff about a car and a bin. I have the words, but I don't think I *know* them. Not really."

"I'll explain it all to you when the time comes."

"When will that be?"

"It may never be," I told her, calling on my patience. "But if we return to those women, that will be the time. All right?"

The child nodded vigorously. Then she looked up at me. "That's our contract, isn't it?"

"I just told you—"

"—*Our* contract," she said. "Yours and mine."

It was my turn to nod.

Then we walked.

"Why are we going this way?" the child asked, hours later.

"Which way is that?"

"I don't *know,* do I? But it isn't the *same* way. You know. You know exactly what I mean. The same way that those runes showed us."

"You have that word now?"

"Don't I?"

"I believe you do. And we are walking a different path because we are looking for something different."

"Not the cartographer?"

"Another word for you," I acknowledged, respectfully.

"Not truly. I remember things very good, don't I? But that doesn't mean I understand them all. So...?"

"So ... what?"

"So what is a cartographer?"

"A maker of maps."

"We need someone to make us a map?"

"Yes."

"A map away from here?"

"Yes."

"That would be good," the child said, as if approving of my search for the first time.

I went into silence.

"It tastes different," the child said that evening, after a bite of the ball of yellowcake.

"But still good?"

"Oh, yes. But why is it different?"

"Confidence."

"Confidence. That means when you're sure of something."

"Yes."

"I still don't—"

"—Because you aren't the same kind of hungry you once were," I explained, ignoring her reversion to "Why?" Or perhaps giving in to it. "Now, you know that when you are hungry, there will be food. So the food you eat, it tastes differently."

"So ... wait! I know. Your cigarette, it always tastes the same?"

"No."

"Because you know you *can't* get the cigarette anytime you want?"

"That's right," I said. I didn't take it farther down that same road. How to explain to a child that cigarettes taste differently after sex? Then the thought that this was a child who might actually understand suddenly intruded, and I had to call on Patience to keep the red-mottled black mist off my spirit.

The new path was a tributary off the river of earth we had been walking. Narrower. With far less human traffic. Some spots we passed were thick with residents, heavy with dealers, traders, and buyers, ringed by promising guides and thieves waiting for their moment. Like the Sector, but with only ground-level units. And a visible sky.

"The cartographer won't be here," the child said.

"How do you know?"

"I'm confident," she said, a smile ghosting her mouth.

"Very good."

"Anyway, we don't care about that. Not now. We're looking for the Fourth, aren't we?"

"Yes."

"I know how to find her."

"You?"

"I ... think so. We have to look for people like.... Wait! Not people. I don't know what to call ... people like Rem and Lo. And Gret. I don't know what to call them."

"You can call them 'people,'" I told her. "You and me, we'll know the difference. It doesn't matter if anyone else does."

"A secret?" she asked. I didn't see her mouth tremble, but I felt it clear enough.

"No. Not a secret. Just because somebody doesn't know something, that doesn't make it a secret." I spent a

spell-word, then held out a closed fist. "Do you know what's in my hand?"

"More yellowcake?"

"No."

"One of your spikes?"

"No."

"The red powder?"

"No."

"That ... dust?"

"No."

"Then.... I don't know."

I opened my hand. The cocoon inside parted. The child watched, rapt, as the black-and-white gynandro butterfly waited for its wings to dry in the new light. When it finally took off, she clapped her hands.

"I didn't know what was in your hand. But that wasn't a secret, it was a pretty thing."

"Sometimes, it is. Sometimes, it isn't. Before I showed you the powder, before I explained what the Seismic Dust was for, before I threw the spike, you didn't know any of that, either, did you? That's how life works. What you don't know, you can learn. What you *do* know, that's called 'knowledge.' There are millions of things you don't know. But those things aren't secrets."

"Do you know all those things?"

"Everybody knows something. Nobody knows everything."

"Yes!" she said, the trembling inside her gone.

For now.

"When are we going to look?" the child asked, later.

"We are looking."

"But I told you—"

"—I remember," I assured her. "But we can't look into certain places without people looking at us."

"If we can't look, how could we find anything?"

"We don't need our eyes to look," I said. "But that's not for now. We have to walk a long way yet. And it's getting dark."

"You should be sleeping," I told the child. "And don't ask 'Why?' I already explained that to you. Children need sleep to help them grow. Don't you want to grow?"

"I do."

"You're so sure?"

"Oh, yes."

"Because...?"

"It's not good to be small. People ... I can say that for all of them, now ... 'people,' right? People can hurt you when you're small."

"When you're big, too."

"I know. I mean, I saw you...."

"Some children are safe. Grown people—adults, I know you have that word—they protect those children."

"Adults like you?"

"No," I said. Thinking of Sector parents who risked everything, every single day, just to keep their young ones safe. Thinking of the Synthetic Woman reclaiming her possession. "'Parents,' that's a word you know?"

"Yes. It means people who have babies. Not just people, either. Cats can have babies. Those are called kittens...."

She started to cry then. I draped a blanket around her, held it against the cold until she fell asleep.

"Does that help you think?"

"The cigarette?"

"Yes."

"I don't know. I can think without a cigarette, that much I *do* know," I told her, forcefully pushing my thoughts away from a place where a worthless cigarette

could be worth a human life. Prison math: the more contraband the product, the more its value.

"We have a lot of ... tasks, don't we?" she said through a full mouthful of yellowcake.

"Not so many."

"We have to find the Fourth, don't we? And then the cartographer?"

"Yes, we do," I agreed, wondering when it became "we," but not pursuing the thought. Focusing on the contract the child didn't know about. Knowing something was there, but not ready to test, yet.

"I have to leave you here," I told the child.

"Leave me? You mean—"

"Only for a while," I said, handing her the two glass globes. "If you stay still, no one will bother you."

"But if—"

"If anyone comes inside the circle—the dust we sprinkled, remember?—just drop these on the ground," I told her, handing her two glass balls. "One will ... keep everyone away; the other will tell me something happened, and I'll come back."

"How long will you be gone?"

"I don't know. There's plenty of yellowcake in the

pack. There's clean water in that pool from the rock-drip. You can study your words until I return, all right?"

"I ... I don't know."

"What don't you know?"

"How do I know you'll come back?"

"I could have left you anytime I wanted, yes? I could have just walked away while you were asleep."

The child went silent while I smoked my cigarette. She didn't ask for a taste.

Finally, she sat down next to me. "You could have sold me, too," she said.

That's when I knew I could ask her about memory.

But not then. The time was wrong. I could ask her only when I made it all *dead* wrong.

As I walked, I thought it through, using a method I'd learned in Iso, hanging a whiteboard on the wall of my mind. Writing down what I knew. What I wanted. Intersecting the lines. Turning the maps into 3-D. Stepping through one to another, the way I'd crossed buildings as a boy. Before Edger tried to teach me to fly.

The Sector is a labyrinth of crossroads. The power of a crossroads lies in the choices each offers. But for those who refuse to choose, standing in the crossroads becomes

standing in a sniper's crosshairs. I had been obeying my mantra before I could say it in words:

You stand still, you get caught.

You run, you get tired.

So....

Learn to lie.

Then learn to lie in wait.

I made a list. My only one:

I wanted to cross the Membrane forever, wanted to live in the City as a Full-Clear.

A common Sector dream, achieved by few. If achieved at all. If anyone was truly living as a Full-Clear, they hadn't re-crossed to boast of it.

Entrance was easy, staying was the opposite. Unless you had the key. That key: all kinds of rumors, myths, legends, tales, lies. I'd tried some, talked with those who tried others. But a life of survival in the Sector, crossing the Membrane to break City law for pay, always returning ... that life had taught me only two truths for the Sector-born:

Magick is real, but the Membrane blocks it, protecting the City.

and:

Money was the only answer to all my questions.

What did that leave?

I first did that math inside City Prison, after I'd gone to the end of the Dark White trail and come up empty.

Now, I wanted that money. Wanted what I risked for, waited for. *Paid* for.

That money was somewhere in the City.

And, somewhere in the Sector, there was a map to that money.

Where else *could* it be? Dark White had operated in the City—the armored cars, the banks—but its roots were all Sector-born, and the map had to be hidden beyond the reach of City law.

The money itself, that wouldn't be in the Sector. The stolen cash had been pop-sealed in rectangular cubes of hundreds, with pull-tabs to open each one. The cubes were stored in heavy canvas sacks, individually padlocked, then cross-chained. Somewhere in the City.

It wouldn't be in the Pure Zone—paper currency had no value there.

So.... a map hidden in the Sector, but leading to somewhere in the City.

Only the cartographer or the Synthetic Woman could show me where that map was hidden. If I found the cartographer, he'd tell me. And even if he was gone, the Synthetic Woman could scour the Sector until it turned up.

There was no reason for the Synthetic Woman to cheat me—money didn't mean a thing to her, wouldn't change her life in any way. In the Sector, she was perfection. In the City, she was product. In the Pure Zone, she was powerless.

And so the contract.

I began by looking for flags. Dark White would have its own, although I wasn't sure I'd recognize it. But, in the Pure Zone, where each lived as they truly were, I'd know those whose markings I falsely wore.

It took me three full twenty-fours to accept that I wouldn't find their flag. And still another to return to where I'd left the child.

"You have to wear this from now on," I told her the next morning, holding out the small leather cuff connected to a length of chain that I'd brought back with me. Part of my harvest. City gangsters use biodegradable plastic bags when they bury bodies—that way they can decompose down to skeletons while keeping carrion-eaters ... and the police ... at a distance. In the Pure Zone,

there's no need for such. I'd left the corpse of the slaver in the field where we'd met. Next to the pair of sloppy bodyguards he'd brought with him.

"I know what this is," she said, displaying no fear.

"So you know what it *really* is, then?"

"A ... ruse!"

"That's some word. Are you sure you—"

"—A ruse is a trick. A ... a false impression that you give to fool someone."

"Yes. The chain around your wrist is a ruse. Also, a disguise."

"Like you're going to sell me?"

"*Just* like that."

"But I know you're not."

"You don't want to *show* anyone you know."

"How would I do that?"

"If you were bouncing around like you do when you're excited. Or if you're smiling, all happy, or—"

"—Oh, I know that."

"All right," I told her, getting ready to travel. "Do you remember the word I explained to you. 'Trustworthy?' And how many different ways that could be?"

"Yes."

"Remember our contract? The different words we were promised if we bring those women their Fourth?"

"Yes. But I don't know the—"

"—I only know one of them. The one they had to give me in case I would need it when we find their Fourth."

"The snap-the-lock word!"

"Yes," I said, kneeling beside her. "Come close." And I whispered that word to her.

The child couldn't cover ground as quickly as I could, and several times I had to deliberately slow down to keep her from trying.

"We're in no hurry," I told her. "We don't know where we're going, only what we're looking for."

"But if we don't—"

"—You see those people coming toward us?"

"Yes."

"That happens along every road. People come toward us, people come from behind us. And people come across our path, too. So if we move too quickly, we might miss some of those."

"Then we could just stay here and wait, couldn't we?"

"We could. But then we couldn't change our path if we wanted to."

"Why would we want to?"

"Because we're looking for.... This is difficult to

explain. What we want is an intersection. Do you have—"

"—Crossroads! Like you said when we found those runes. Crossroads, right?"

"Absolutely right," I assured her. Feeling calm flood my being. Not calm because I knew where to find it, calm because I knew how to look.

I did, now.

To everyone we passed who looked as if they might know, I asked the same question, made the same offer. I had the product. I wanted the source.

Throughout every such encounter, the child's face was a bland mask, as if she'd been drugged into a walking stupor.

Some fled. Some showed contempt. Some attempted to take what I'd offered for the information I sought by trick or by force. Occasionally, some would attempt to rescue my captive. For those, the remedy was not my skills or my tools, it was the child's own words.

Days passed before I picked up a tendril, tugged on it until I felt it pulse with life, and followed its path.

The row was all flesh peddlers. Some of the merchandise was chained, all of that for sale. Some was roaming loose—volunteers, or so their owners said. Those could be rented, but not taken off the grounds.

Behind the cages, an Inspection Station. Buyers brought their own medicos, the bulk purchasers brought their own haulers.

Guards watched alertly. Not for liberation forces like they have in the Sector—for de-gens who wanted to see flesh in cages but didn't have the resources to actually buy their own. No look-tourists allowed.

The child chained to me was my ID card, the currency I displayed at the gate was proof of its validity.

We passed without challenge, until a woman wearing a surgical mask held up her hand for us to halt.

"You seek ... what?"

"My property," I answered her.

"Whatever is here—"

"—I am not here to reclaim," I cut her off. "If my property is here, I will buy it back from its current owner."

"Describe your property."

"What good would that do? It's been almost three years," I answered, leaving words about changes that could be created—or inflicted—unsaid.

"We don't buy here," she said, looking directly at the

child.

"I am not selling."

"A trade, then?"

"No."

Finally, she shrugged her shoulders slightly. I took it for passage permission.

"She wasn't there?" the child said, when we were an hour past the flesh market.

"No."

"That's why you had to see their eyes?"

"Yes."

"Are you angry at me?"

"No. Why would you think that?"

"Your hand. The one I held when we were walking through there. Your hand went cold. Like ice, only it burned."

"I was.... I was worried about you. Seeing all that...."

"I saw it before," she said. Not trying for emotionlessness, simply matter-of-fact. "Not all at once, like here. But ... people, people I guess, would come past my post. Sometimes, they had those cages. On wheels. With donkeys pulling them. Or maybe burros, or mules. I don't know which. I have the words, but not the pictures

to go with them. I don't have that ... encyclopedia you told me about, so sometimes it's hard to make them match."

"It would be hard for me, too," I told her, consciously moving away from what we'd both just seen. "They have mules in the City, to pull people through parks, but—"

"—What's the City?"

"It's just a place. From here, you would cross a river, then be in another place. If you crossed through *that* place, you would be in the City."

"Oh."

I let that word hang in the air between us as we walked.

"I've never been to the City," she said, that evening.

"Maybe, someday, you'll—"

"—I've never been anyplace, except—"

"Do you want some yellowcake," I cut in, not wanting to hear what she was going to say.

"—except with you," she finished, as if I hadn't interrupted.

I tried to let it go. Tried to deal with it as I'd learned to deal with pain. Never with power, always with technique.

Let it pass through, don't allow it to stay. Breathe it out.

None of that worked.

"Remember when you were talking about ... your post, yesterday?"

"I wasn't."

"When cages would come by? Pulled by—"

"—Oh! That wasn't about.... I mean, it's just where I *was* when I would see them."

"You have a good memory."

"I think I do. But no one ever said."

"You have the word."

"Yes. But that doesn't always help me see."

"Like with mules and donkeys and burros."

"Yes! I know what a memory is, so I know what a *good* one would be, but I don't really know how to tell."

I thought about my cigarette—did some shallow breath-exchanges, instead. "Do you have 'year' for a word?"

"Yes. But it's just like those others."

"What others?"

"The ones you've been *saying*," the child pouted.

"You know what it means, but you can't see it?"

"That's right. I wish I could see...."

"Do you know how old you are?"

"That's in years. I know that's in years. But I don't

know how *many* years, so...."

I wished I knew a word for "remember," but all I knew were synonyms, so the path wouldn't be any easier.

Maybe the cigarette would help.

I let the child have a harmless puff. She never seemed to want more than one.

"Before you worked at your post...."

"Before?"

"Yes. There were other children, remember?"

"Oh. Them. I remember. Because they were there first."

"Yes. You came after them. Because they were there were first. But then they were gone."

"Yes, they were—"

"—Sssshh," I cut her off. "Did any other children come later? After you?"

"Oh, no. They needed more, but they wanted a good bargain. Gret said I had lot of days left, so they didn't have to make a bargain they didn't want. Not in a hurry, she would say."

I knew there hadn't been other children beyond that portal. A child with this one's heart—the kitten she sent over to spare it pain; the traxxyls she'd screamed at to save from poisoning—such a child would never have left little ones behind. And if there had been younger ones who'd

been Gret's version of "bad," I didn't need to make her talk about that.

"Do you …" I spit the words out, keeping my voice flat as a shield against its thorns, "Do you remember when you first came to that place?"

"I was always there," she said.

Maybe that's when the tiles started to drop, the mosaic forming on the screen in my mind.

"We have to see her for ourselves, don't we?" the child asked. "That's why we never ask about her?"

"That's right."

"Because we don't really know what she looks like."

"Just the eyes."

"Yes. But aren't those … special? Wouldn't anyone who saw eyes like they told you about, wouldn't they … remember?"

"They didn't say, but it seems that this woman … their Fourth … she can control her eyes. The same way those three we met do. And she would know not to show that to others."

"How will she know to show it to us, then?"

"This is just a guess, you have that word, 'guess'? Good. Just a guess, but there must be a way for those women to

tell their Fourth that I'm coming for her."

"We are."

"I just said—"

"—Not you," the child corrected me. "Us. You and me. We're coming for her."

She wasn't in any of the depths we searched. The just-below-ground marketplaces were always marked at their entrances, but never guarded. I knew how that worked. It was the same in the Sector: No guards, no passports, no entry fee. Once outsiders entered, it was up to them to find their own way from there. No maps available, but every few steps would bring opportunities. Some call those chances. Others call them risks.

That always depended on why they came. And what they came for.

There was flesh down there, too. But not even close to what we were seeking.

"Are we lost?" the child asked, one time.

"No," Is all I answered. How to explain to her that the Sector-born all navigated by pulse? That the throbbing wouldn't keep you out of the danger if you went down the wrong path, but it would always lead you back to where you started if you obeyed its call? The "lifeline," the old

ones called it.

Two men followed us out of the last tunnel. Followed at a distance all the way to where we made camp. I let them come—I had to learn if they were the actual crew, or just scouts.

That night, they came.

I hadn't needed the Seismic Dust. Hadn't been asleep.

But I'd taken precautions. Even if they had been able to leave, they would have left without the child they'd come for.

Five days later, the child asked: "What if we can't find her? The Fourth?"

I shrugged. Not dismissing her question ... not knowing the answer.

"But we have a contract, don't we?"

"There's all kinds of contracts," I told her. "This isn't a promise contract; it's a trade contract."

"What's the—"

"—A promise contract is if I tell you I am going to do something, I have to do it. If you give your word, you have to keep your word."

"Always?"

"Always."

"People lie," she said, solemnly.

"Some do," I agreed.

"So their contracts...?"

"For those people, those people who lie, their contracts are no good."

"I don't—"

"—The word of a liar has no value. So it can't be traded for anything."

"The trade contract!"

I took out my cigarette to buy a little time. The child's patience held.

"A trade contract is what we have. With those women. For their Fourth. I promised to look for her. And I *am* looking. If—"

"—*We* are!"

"Yes. All right, we are. We promised to look for that woman, and we *are* doing that, aren't we? If, *if* we find her, *if* we bring her to those women, *then* they will give us what they promised. But as a trade, you see?"

"So our contract is we have to *try*?"

"Yes."

"Only try?"

"Yes. We could not promise to find their Fourth. She may not be anywhere we look. Or she could be...."

"Dead."

"Yes."

"How long do we try?"

"Until we know we have done our best," I told her, hoping she was out of questions. At least for a while.

We encountered many travelers, but questioned none of them. Simply answering *their* questions gave us all the information we could have extracted, and most were content to inquire about prospects we might have passed on the road behind us.

"We have to look for more cages," the child said, one morning.

I nodded to indicate she was correct. If their Fourth was free, she would be moving toward the Faiths on her own, and we hadn't come across any woman traveling in that direction. Some of the smaller caravans had women, but they all seemed to have roles to play, and none of them had looked like captives. Still, I always checked their eyes.

We didn't travel with the child chained to me, just attached it when any group that might be peddlers approached.

If it hadn't been for the flag, we might have passed by the small compound without a second glance. But the white banner wasn't a sign for truce or peace, not with the red-and-black lightning bolts slashed as a message across it.

I never changed pace, so neither did the child.

That night, we camped close by.

She didn't ask her "Why?" Not even when I sprinkled the dust around our perimeter and faded into the night.

"Was she there?" the child asked when I returned.

"I don't know," I told her. "She might be. But I can only look in daylight. And I can't take you with me when I do."

"What if—"

"—Nobody will find you alone," I said. "We'll walk tomorrow. And find a place for you to stay. A safe place."

She was quiet for a long time. But her breathing told me she was avoiding sleep.

"What is it?" I said, very softly.

"Remember when you asked me.... Remember when you asked me if I ... remembered?"

"Yes," I said, carefully.

"I remember *some* things. At least, I *think* I do. Just ... feeling things, not actually *seeing* them, you know?"

"The way a baby—"

"—I wasn't a baby," she cut me off.

"Everyone was once a—"

"—I know I *was* a baby," she whispered, as if telling a secret. "I just don't ... remember *being* a baby. It was like being asleep. And when I woke up, there she was."

"Gret."

"Gret," she affirmed. "Isn't it like that for everyone?"

"I don't know," I told her, honestly.

"You?"

"I don't understand what you're—"

"—Do *you* remember being a baby?"

"No," I told her, telling her the truth. "No, I don't."

The next morning, my mind was clear of all but two things. Two things in one: a gynandro. A bisected bullet— half hardball, half dum-dum.

Find the Fourth.

and:

A woman. More ... maybe three, four women. I'm ... squirming. Not crying. Something on my skin. "He will have scars," one of them said.

"I'm going to have some people around this spot," I told the child. "Just to keep intruders away."

"Won't the Dust—"

"The Dust is for warning, not for repelling."

"But what if the people you get are bad people?"

"They might be bad people," I acknowledged. "But they won't do anything bad to you."

"But you won't *be* here."

"I'm going to tell you two words. You might think you have those words, but you don't ... not the way they would be used. One word will blaze a wall of fire around you, but if you sit quietly, it won't burn you. The other word will call me."

"How long will the fire blaze?"

"Until I return."

The child nodded. "Tell me the words," she said.

I told her the word to call for fire. Then I said, "The other word is my name. It will always call me to you."

"Is that the word I think I know?"

"Carbon," I said. "Do you have that word?"

"I have it now," the child answered, closing her eyes to sleep. "And I know what it means."

I didn't allow the contract to infect my patience. Sooner or later, they would come. The City, the Sector, the Pure Zone ... they have separators between them, but always some of the same things inside—people who can be hired. No claim of a higher purpose, no pretense of loyalty. Some like the work; some want the payment. Mercenaries aren't all alike, but they all have the same core.

It was four days before they came. Three men, two women, a heavily-laden cart, pulled by two mules. They didn't have a flag, but the weapons they carried were just as clear.

"The work is to camp here," I told the woman who stepped toward me first.

"Camp?"

"Camp and guard."

"Guard what?"

"Someone just inside that copse, the one with the red leaves."

"Just one?"

"It doesn't matter," I said. "No one enters. That's the job."

"For how long?"

"Until I return."

"That could be—"

"—No more than twenty-one days. It could be much less."

"And you'll pay...?"

"Currency."

"By the day?"

"If you wish."

"What else is there?"

"A flat fee. If what you are to protect is safe when I return, I will pay you a fair price. A price *you* set."

"Would you go to—"

"—A price you set," I repeated.

The woman turned her back and walked a few paces over to the others in her band. The conversation was animated but quiet—their gestures had no meaning I could translate.

The price was too ridiculous to be anything but a test.

"I will not play bargaining games," I told her, very formal. "You have a true price, one you will actually accept. There is no reason to reach this by steps toward some imaginary mid-point. Tell me your true price, and I will say 'yes' or 'no.' Either way, we will be finished. If you say 'yes,' your work begins with my departure."

She told me their price.

"I will pay that. If I return and all is as agreed, you will be paid at that moment."

"You offer nothing as a ... deposit?"

"My word. My promise. You know I must return, as what you guard is precious to me."

"What if we do our best, but—"

"—If you attempt to learn what is precious to me, to see it for yourselves; if you attempt to hold that preciousness as a hostage for a higher price than we agreed, you will pay the highest of prices."

"You would attack us?" the woman asked, as if genuinely interested. "All of us?"

"I would kill you," I promised. "All of you."

I had purchased twenty-one days, but I gave myself only nine. I calculated that I could return more quickly than I would be traveling, but that would only be if I moved alone. If I found the Fourth, she might slow my return steps, so I added in those extra days.

As a child in the Sector, I learned if you wanted things—food, shelter, excitement ... sometimes, even air itself—there would always be risk. As I learned different skills, I learned those skills always shared an essence—reducing some risk. Only fools believed that any level of

skill, any mastery of technique, any charm or spell could make risk disappear. Fools are often tolerated, but their lives were sand in random hourglasses.

"Put down the duffel," the compound guard said.

I did that. But when he moved to open it, I shook my head.

"No one brings a sack in here without it being opened," the guard said. "You got to stand for a body-search, too."

As he spoke, two more men appeared behind him.

"Only I can open the sack," I said, casting out calm in waves. "Any other hand on it would bring death."

"Suppose that goes for your body, too," one of the new guards said. He didn't sound afraid, so I knew he wasn't a leader.

I said nothing.

"There's a spell on the sack?" the first guard asked. "Or is it you who's the wizard?"

"There are no spells. And I am no wizard. The sack's protection is planted within its folds and layers."

"And you?"

"I am protected only by my skills."

The guard nodded, as if finally understanding

something very complex. "We don't have the fights except once a week," he said. "And you just missed the last card by a couple of nights."

"I did not come to fight. I have come to buy."

"Buy what?" the third guard asked. Not hostile, not especially interested ... just playing his role.

"A breeder."

"You have enough currency for that?" he asked again, now with a heavily doubtful weight in his voice.

"Yes."

"So where is it?"

"After I see the breeder."

"What makes you think we've got breeders here?"

"The flag."

"Our flag?"

"My flag, too," I told him, as I pulled the cord to drop my garments to the waist.

The first one they sent against me wasn't a test of skill—I killed him seconds after he launched. I figured him for a disposable, one they weren't sure of despite some superficial prove-in. I'd been one of those, once. But I'd moved to another level quickly, as those hunting Dark White closed in.

The one who had given the signal for the launch stepped close to me.

"Your markings are from the other side," he said. Not questioning, stating a fact.

I nodded. Less than a bow, but still respectful.

"Sector or City?"

"Me? Or my ink?"

"Both."

"That is your answer, then."

He put his hands behind his back, as if to assure me I was in no danger from him. A display for the others, nothing more.

"You're saying, a man can't be born in two places, but he can be marked in more than one."

I nodded again. A touch deeper, still short of a bow.

"You came to join us?"

"I came to buy."

"To start your own—"

"—To breed my own," I cut him off. "With my own seed."

He took a step backward, careful to keep his hands behind him. Either a prideful gesture or a foolish one. The kill I'd already done was enough to show him that he'd never reach a belt-concealed weapon in time.

"You could breed in here," he finally said.

"I don't know your ways," I answered. "Not in the Pure Zone, only on the other side."

"We're the same everywhere."

"No, you're not."

"How could you know that?"

"On the other side, no one man can speak for the movement."

"Maybe we have a Triangle here."

"Maybe you do. If that is true, I speak to them, not to you. If it is not, I speak to you."

"Speak to me."

"I won't breed here."

"Why not? Are you not among your brothers, now?"

"I may be. I don't know. But it wouldn't matter. I won't breed here because I will keep the babies. Keep them for myself."

"Not for our movement? Not to be warriors for our race?"

"Not to follow orders from those I don't know."

"Why could you not know us? *Come* to know us?"

"Because I am not staying."

"You already said—"

"—Not staying on this side of the Kangol. Not staying in the Pure Zone."

"Did you not escape from the other side? Come here to

be safe?"

"I came to the Pure Zone seeking purity. To breed pure-to-pure. To continue the struggle."

"The struggle on the other side is over. All our people have been—"

"—And yet here I stand."

"You think we don't have access? That we don't get messages?"

"I hope you do. That would mean that there are others, somewhere. Others who survived the purging."

"There are some such."

"So you say."

"Say your name. If you're telling all true, say your name."

"It's not my name you want. It's the name of what once was."

"Say that, then."

"Dark White."

That she was the fourth of the women they showed me might have been chance. Pure chance in the Pure Zone. Or maybe the Faiths were well-named.

A blonde, but then again, they all were. Blue eyes. And that, too, was common to them all.

When I stood before her, those eyes flashed: Nordic to golden bronze to dark garnet ... held there an extra second, flashed the same color as the blanket used by the Faiths, then back to that Valhalla blue.

"This one," I told the men who had formed a semi-circle behind me. "And that one," I added, pointing out another of the blondes, a much younger one.

"Two?" the spokesman said. Not so much questioning as confirming.

"Two," I answered.

"Why two?"

"Neither has been bred," I said, making a question of my statement, taking the lack of a response for affirmation. "So neither is proven. I must be sure of their fertility—"

"—If you stayed here, and waited for the outcome, you would be sure."

"I will not stay here," I said.

"Why don't you offer to buy all of them, then?"

"I cannot be sure to control more than two. Those cages are not for traveling. Two is the most I can manage. If I do not have at least one child in a year from now, I will return for the others."

There was no bargaining. The women varied in appearance—height, weight, age-by-look—but each carried the same price tag. I pointed out the two I'd picked, then took a couple of steps back.

I dropped to one knee and opened my duffel, motioning the spokesman to come close so I could transfer the payment to his hands. As he came within range, I flung three of the glass balls to the hard ground, spoke two spell-words, and stopped his heart with a viper's strike. I was on my feet before any of them could react.

"I am the Messenger," I orated. "The last of Dark White. We were born in the Sector; we were betrayed in the City. I am the last of our movement, just released from their prison by the same spell I have cast here. I crossed into the Pure Zone to bring breeders back into the Sector. That was my mission.

"For my message, heed this: just as we were betrayed in the City, so you all were to be betrayed by the traitor I have just killed."

They stirred as if to rush me, but that's all it was ... a stirring as the wind stirs high grass, not strong enough to uproot.

"You have women here who came as volunteers. It is only with those women that the movement must grow in the Pure Zone. The captives, I take with me. On this side

of the Kangol, they are cursed—they will take no man's seed."

I could see some of them looking past me. I didn't turn, but I knew what they were seeing—the snap-lock word had opened all the cages, and the four women were standing outside the bars.

"I have used powers that were granted to me by Dark White potioneers, to be used only as we approach the Final Days. You see that mist along the ground? The *white* mist? That is mine to command. I am leaving, now. With the women. Hear me! I can leave you in peace, or I can leave you dead."

I bowed with a show of respect as fraudulent as the brotherhood I was claiming.

As we walked, the Fourth spoke to the other women in a language I didn't know. Not only a language I didn't understand—there are many such throughout the Sector—but one I had never heard spoken.

The first night, one of the women vanished.

The second night, another.

After the third night, it was only me and the Fourth.

She walked strongly. We covered ground quickly. Approaching in daylight, I saw the mercenaries protecting the red-leaved copse.

The child was inside. Alone with her word-book, practicing her patience.

I paid the guards. They accepted wordlessly. We moved away, in different directions.

The Fourth settled into the Faiths so seamlessly that I could no longer see any traces of the Nordic Pure disguise she had adopted to survive. We all sat around their blanket.

"We have read your cards," one said to me. "Now shall we read your markings?"

"Those are—"

"—Not what you believe them to be. Not ...ah, wait; you *have* no beliefs. Yet your markings have meaning, still."

"Not—"

"—Watch the cards," she said, tossing them onto the blanket.

No symbols this time. Three cards. Two eights. One eighty-eight.

"88" was on both my triceps. As it had been on a final-

solution ball on that billiards table. Connected, then, I thought. But I said nothing.

"Eight-by-eight is the number sign for justice and fullness," the card-reader said. "Only in the Pure Zone would they appear so. Perfect equality. Eight and eight together is the same message, expressed differently. The eights are always equal. If divided they are still equal. If divided again, they remain always equal to each other. Say your name. Say your name, now. Say it to us."

"Carbon," was all I had.

"That is a shield name," she said. "Taken to protect you, protecting your true name each time it is spoken."

"So my true name, then?" I asked. For the first time in my life.

"You speak, not as a challenger, but as a seeker. Your true name is the truth of your conduct. What you do *is* your name. Just as what you were *was* your name."

"So I have a new name?"

"Not yet," she said. "But when you say the word we will give to you, you will know your name."

"When I say it?"

"At that moment. But not here. Not now."

"Then...?"

"Your name will come to you when you say the word. But *when* you say the word has no meaning, only *why* you

say it."

She reached out for my hands. Took them in hers, silk over scars. "Quiet your mind," she said.

The word came to me. Not a new word, an added one.

"I won't go," the child said, standing in a fighting stance against an enemy she could not see.

"Yes, you will," I told her. "I'll be with you until transport comes. Then you will go with these women. They will protect you."

"Go *where?*"

"Different places. It doesn't matter. I know where you will end up. And...."

"And what?" she demanded.

"And I'll know where to find you."

"Why can't you come with us?"

"Because, if I did, I wouldn't be able to find you later."

"You promise?"

"I promise."

"Will I get one, too?"

"One what?"

"A name. A new name. Like they said you would get."

"Yes. A new name."

"How will I know? I don't have a name now. Not like

you do."

"You heard what the Faiths said. The name I have now isn't a true name. It is incomplete. I might as well have no name at all."

"Like me."

"Yes. Just like you."

It seemed we reached the Poison Tree very quickly. Our passage was never blocked, no taxes were claimed, no tolls demanded. The Faiths shared my yellowcake without explanation, taking turns holding the child's hand.

Everyone had their role, unrehearsed.

Mine was the watcher who awaited the arrival of the Cargo Car. He never knew what killed him.

A few hours passed.

We watched the Cargo Car cross the Kangol and come to a stop. The driver stepped out and unlatched the back of his vehicle.

All of us approached, me carrying the child, she playing her role. To look at her, she seemed to be sleep-drugged.

The driver unlocked the cage in the back of his vehicle. Children began to stumble out. I handed the child toward the driver. He stepped back, face contorting in disgust.

"I don't touch merchandise," he spat. "Load her

yourself once I've emptied out."

The Faiths stood to one side as the children filed out.

I carried the child to the car and laid her inside. As I stood up, I spun to my right, slipped my left forearm around the driver's neck and drove my right elbow into the side of his face. I locked my left hand over my right biceps, cracked my knee into his spine, and compressed his airway ... the anaconda, come to call.

Some watched him die without a flicker of interest, some looked away.

The Faiths said words. The cage cracked and crumbled. When the back of the Cargo Car was emptied of capture equipment, it seemed much larger.

The Fourth climbed behind the wheel. The child sat between her and one of the other Faiths. The children who had been emptied from the capture cage jumped back into the cavernous opening, excited like they were going to a wonderful circus.

When the Cargo Car was loaded, one of the Faiths spoke to me from a side window.

"The next one is yours," she said. "Yours alone."

I gave it nine suns more in the Pure Zone. Wandering in circles, never far from the Poison Tree. When it was

time, I took up my position. I felt presences, but no one approached. A watcher had to be somewhere close, awaiting the Cargo Car, ignoring all others. When I heard the hum of its motor, I used one of the few words I had left.

The transporter watched me approach. I reached into the vehicle and locked my thumb and fingers into a nerve juncture. I used the word to unsnap the cage in the back.

"We're going across the other way," I told him. "All of us."

"I can't return with a load. They'll—"

"—You're going to drop this whole load in the Sector," I said. "Me included. Then you're going back to your depot, empty."

"But they'll know the cargo was never delivered. They can check with the—"

"—The man who was supposed to do the pickup at this end is dead. His body hasn't been moved. What they'll think is that the cargo got hijacked."

"What if they don't believe me? They'll kill me. That's not right. I didn't do—"

"—They'll believe you," I promised him. "Even if they put you on the machine, all you have to do is tell the truth. The truth, understand? Your load *was* hijacked. That *is* the truth."

"You can't drive a Cargo Car," he bargained. "It takes a special ... I'm not saying. But I know you already know you can't be a driver. That's why you need me."

"I don't need you," I told him, thinking how the Faiths had truly needed their Fourth. "I can just kill you and wait for the next car. I'm a very patient man."

"What choice do I have?"

My silence was his answer.

The Synthetic Woman had the Sector wired, but I had deeper roots than hers, and mine were home-grown, not conjured from chemicals.

The child had been delivered to her, along with whatever story the Faiths concocted. A story that said the man she contracted with was dead.

The Synthetic Woman would believe that last part. After all, I hadn't come with the child, and I'd never showed up to claim my end of the contract. What she didn't know: I'd slipped through the Sector, down into the tunnels, and finally across the Membrane.

I wasn't worried the child would tell her anything—she wouldn't be asked.

But I knew I'd only get the one chance to make it all

work.

"You found me easy enough, mahn. Did you find what you promised, too?"

"Not yet," I told the undercover. Words I'd been using way too much lately whenever I talked to myself.

"So what is the plan?"

"He's here, on this side," I said, with a certainty I didn't feel. "The Sector might be his birth-home, but he's not welcome there. Or safe. The Sector keeps secrets from your side of the Membrane, but inside it, there's no such protection. And there's that reward, too. You have your laws here, but those restrain you, chain you even more than they do those you want to control."

"Who is this 'you,' mahn? You think I am a Power here?"

"No," I told him. "But I might be."

"You sound crazy," he said, eyes sweeping my upper body. "You changed your ink?"

"Did I?"

"I ... I am not certain. Your arms ... where is the ... wait! Let me see the spider web."

I brought my left fist to my cheekbone.

"It is not the same."

"You mean the little spider that's there now?"

"Mahn, when is the last time you looked in a mirror?"

Two nights later, we met in an alley. A much wider one than any in the Sector, plenty of space to allow a disposal truck to make regular stops on a route.

"I am taking a big risk, mahn."

"More than you know."

"More? You are such an insane white man, I am surprised your mouth does not foam. What more could there be than to steal those records you say will lead us to the killer?"

"The risk is that I'm right. The killer does what he does for a reason. Remember what I told you? What I learned? He's not a rapist, not a pyro, not any kind of de-gen. Unless you consider an assassin to be in that group."

"Yes, you said all that before. But these records ... you don't believe he's in there, do you? These are some of the City's highest—"

"—*He* won't be in there."

"Then...?"

"A hitman is a hired man. The fire wasn't to keep you from ID'ing the body, and it wasn't to destroy rape signs, either. Women who sell their bodies know better than to

cyber their trick books. They go Old School with that info—at least the high-end ones do."

"So whoever paid for that killing...?"

"Yes. I might be only guessing the hitman is here, but it's a good guess. He may be Sector-born, but he's got a friend on this side. A boss, anyway."

"That's why you only wanted assassins who worked both sides of the Membrane?"

"It is."

"So what's the key, then?"

"It's in here," I said, taking out my case ace and laying it on the lid of a garbage can. "The girl who was killed, she worked as 'Mai Zelle.'"

"It's *her* book we need? You said the fire—"

"—Not her own book, the copy. Another girl had that, just like Mai Zelle had hers. They were friends. Or, at least, they knew each other. Because they worked the same tricks."

"Clients, you mean?"

"No. Tricks they did. Tricks the client needed done."

"What—"

"—Special stuff. Stuff the client couldn't buy on this side without more risk than he could stand. So that's one of the search criteria—our man, a *rich* man, a man of power. He'll be a frequent tourist. His pass-across will be

hologrammed, like any City-born. He has to go where they have what he wants. What he needs. And that will all be in there. In his records, I mean.

"So don't search by name, search by freakishness. And don't pretend you don't keep track that way. Don't act like the only de-gens you have marked down are the ones you lock up."

"We only want the killer."

"And I only want to keep my bargain."

He took out a pack of cigarettes. The box was orange-and-black banded, a brand I didn't recognize. Nodding his head, he held out the box to me.

I stood behind the cop. He was seated across from the man we'd come to meet. The office was a deep pie-slice, a narrow door opening into an ever-widening slab of floor-to-ceiling glass, bare walls. A true man of power doesn't keep his credentials in framed certificates.

"I've never met a detective before," the man said.

"Things work out as they should, you will never meet another one, sir."

"Doesn't your partner want to sit?"

"I'm good where I stand," I told him, robot-voiced.

"Well, then?" the man said. Not impatient, not

anxious. But not disinterested—the phone call to his secret cell phone had made sure of that.

"There was a fire," I told him, like I was reading a news bulletin. "A prostitute was raped and killed—the fire was set to disguise the crimes."

"Yes?"

"The killer is who we want."

"Certainly. That's your job, isn't it? But why—"

"—The killer is *all* we want," I interrupted, letting the words hang between us like a frozen rope. A rope I could thaw and strangle him with if he made the wrong choice.

"We just want the man who hired you," I told the killer, late that same night.

"You don't have—"

"—You're very good," I stopped him from telling us a story. "One of the very, very best. Those loaded cigarette butts, the fire, the de-gens who are supposed to be on the run, the one you left alive in no condition to run.... All that, a masterpiece, no doubt."

"That's just some—"

That's when I told him the name of the man who had contracted the job. The man of power.

"Don't go all stupid on us, now," the cop warned him.

"How do you think we found you? He's already given you up, right down to your coordinates. But you're nothing to us. Just a man doing a job. If it wasn't you, it would have been someone else. Far as we are concerned, you're just the pistol—he's the one who aimed it. The one who pulled the trigger. Understand me?"

The hitman's eyes flicked between us. If he had any chances, he didn't fancy them.

"I'm not dealing," he said. "I walk into a courtroom and I'm—"

"—You have it backwards, fool," the cop told him. "You *don't* walk into a courtroom and you're dead minutes after we walk out that door. This place is being watched. By his people. And our people are watching *them*. You couldn't be more surrounded if you were a coffin in a graveyard. The man who hired you, he's not out of money. He gave us your name to spare his own. That's the City deal. You know how that song goes: one goes down, the other goes free."

"Spell it out," the hitman said, shifting gears inside himself.

"You testify and you walk," the cop said. "But you can't come back here. Ever. Take whatever you can carry, no more. You can't hide in the Sector forever, so it's the Pure Zone for you. What you do once you get there, how you

get by, that's on you."

"And what do I have to do for all that? What do I have to do, exactly?"

"Your turn to spell it out," I told him, tapping the "record" button. "Beginning to end."

"So you don't change your story later," the cop added as he set up the broadcast-quality recorder, a handheld with a pull-out stand and wide-scope mic.

And he did. He hadn't left out a single detail, as if each word was splattering antiseptic over his own hands.

When he saw the cop reach for the recorder, the assassin said, "Don't you want the others I did? Might as well make it a complete—"

I pulled a Frankenstein and the hired killer went quiet. I walked around behind him as the cop switched the camera angle. The assassin took his last breath as I cranked off three quick shots, two into the chair the cop slid out of, one into the sleeve of the coat he'd left behind. Then the cop shot him at the bridge of his nose.

The sound recorder would have all that before we shut it off. I pressed the dead man's hand around the Frankenstein's grip, placed his finger inside the trigger guard, got enough print to pass inspection, then flung the

pistol aside as if from the hand of a freshly-killed.

Then I took off my surgical gloves.

With time running hard against me, I had to fight for my Patience. But I reached deep and gripped it, squeezing relentlessly.

Why kill a whore? I kept asking myself. But I didn't like any of the answers. Not because I'm a moralist. Or a vigilante. Because I needed all the blood spatter to collect into something I could grab and hold onto.

It has to connect, became my mantra. Belief wasn't necessary, only relentlessness.

The one person who I knew could find all the threads was the one person I couldn't ask. I could only go to her the one time, and I needed a different thread pulled when I did.

So I took the long way around.

The *Apex Predator's* interior still pounded. The suicide singer remembered me. It took a "7" compression this time, but we got there. And made our bargain.

The bcc: climbed for me again. This time down,

dropping into the catacombs to reach a cyber crew they traded with, taking me along.

The website that crew tracked down had an alternate-access program. Its back-channel, cross-Membrane URL changed every eight hours. I tried to explain what I was looking for to the girl wearing separate little magnifiers over the lenses of her tinted glasses, but I couldn't find words she understood. I'd know it if I saw it, was all I could finally say to her.

It took almost a week of nights. I had to glaze my eyes and steel my stomach, but I stayed patient. And relentless.

As soon as I saw the "Ultimate Invader Experience," I knew. The price was stunning, but understandably so— none of the three women advertised could be used again for at least eighteen months post-release ... the cost of hospitalization and reconstructive surgery was included.

"No Finales!" the sub-site warned. "Strictly Monitored."

The thread back to the man of power was twisted fiber-optic, the strands color-appropriate.

The site's services included advanced safety features. As soon as its medical team verified actual survival, it went to auto-delete, full scrub. The man of power trusted systems, not people. A program could live, but Layne Violette had to die. And not at the hands of any post-

recovery client.

"You have finally come for your map," the Synthetic Woman said, her voice as assured as her future.

"For that, yes."

"You speak as if there was more."

"More for me," I told her truthfully. "Not for you. I've come for only what's mine."

She told me where the map was.

"Come," I told the child.

"She's not yours," the Synthetic Woman said. "And don't try any spell- words you brought back with you—they won't work here."

As I said the word the Faiths had given me, I learned my name.

Maybe just before she died, the Synthetic Woman knew she'd been wrong twice.

The detective wouldn't take any of the money I knew would be there. Good thing, that. Because now I needed enough for two passports, two Full-Clears.

I offered my hand. He refused it with a "Not just yet..."

gesture.

But he listened. And handed me his orange-and-black cigarette box.

"I'm a businessman," the man of power said, behind the desk in his pie-slice office, speaking to the cop. "I understand commerce. I understand value. The news wire said something about a vicious killer you tracked down. A rapist. And an arsonist, too. A full confession, and then he tried to kill *you*. You're a hero, now. Decorated. Promotion. All well-deserved."

The cop didn't respond. And I wasn't there to speak.

"I'd consider it a privilege to provide my own reward for such heroism," the man of power said. "A significant reward. But a one-time reward, yes?"

The cop nodded, still not speaking.

"I wouldn't want to see you again," the man of power said, as he tapped the combination to his wall safe. "Or hear from you. Do we understand one another, my friend?"

"Oh yes," the cop said, spreading his hands to draw the target's eyes as I closed in.

"Should we ever cross paths again, I won't know you," the cop said later that night. "Your ink ... I don't know what happened, but I can't see it anymore. And your face, that I have already forgotten."

"Fair enough," I said. "I won't know you, either."

He offered his hand. I took it. Even if his hand had been clay, my prints wouldn't ID me. But it felt like flesh. True flesh.

"I'm going to stay with you?" the child asked.

"Yes."

"In this place?" she asked. Her word-book had no name for the Sector. Not yet.

"In this place, yes. But if something happens to me, you'll be able to stay in the other place."

"I don't want to go back to—"

"—Not there," I promised. "Not ever. I mean the place I took you to visit last week. The City, remember?"

"Oh yes! It's very nice there. So many—"

"—Listen to me. The City, that's a place to visit, not to stay. The only ones allowed to stay have special papers. Those cost a lot of money. We're going to buy you those papers. If anything happens to me, those people I brought you to stay with—"

"—The climbers!"

"Yes, those people. You could stay with them, or you could stay with people in the City. It would be your choice."

"I would—"

"—You don't know what you would do," I said. "Not yet, you don't. The papers, those are to give you a *choice*, understand? That's a word you know. I word you know *now*, yes?"

She nodded, her eyes full of understanding and trust.

"The tests will be back in three hours," the woman in the nurse's outfit said. "We have to record DNA before we change the retinal—"

"—Why did you have to run mine?" I cut off her canned recital. "I'm only buying the one set of papers. For the child."

"So she is to be adopted?"

I didn't answer. But the woman wasn't to be put off.

"You're her father, are you not? That was what you told—"

"—I am her father," I confirmed, unworried about the child's reaction ... we had prepared for the interviews together.

"We can sell you a passport," the transactor in the expensive suit said, later. But not for the child."

"Why is that?" I said, feeling the calm-before-kill settle into me. *Was the child the true daughter of the Synthetic Woman? An artificial life-form, created from real flesh?*

"Because she is City-born," the man said. "A Full-Clear at birth. Confirmed by the retinal scan. You, however—"

My mind ran wild until I brought it under control. *The child wasn't an artificial, she was purchased property. Children are sold from the Sector all the time, but they can't be sold within it. The Synthetic Woman had never given birth. She'd bought the child. But not from the Pure Zone—traffic only goes in one direction—from the City.*

"—I know," I told him, calming my heartbeat to polygraph mode, instantly reacting as if I'd expected the DNA results he was holding. "And you already have my money."

"What names shall we enter?"

"You need both?"

"They should already have explained that to you. A birth certificate must have a birth chain. And you said you and the child are related...."

The Faiths had told me true. From the moment I put

forces in motion to reclaim the child from the Synthetic Woman, I had known.

"Blue is my name," I told the transactor. "Karbon Blue. And this is my daughter, Blossom. Blossom Diamond Blue."

CPSIA information can be obtained
at www.ICGtesting.com
Printed in the USA
LVHW061210031119
636178LV00009B/137/P

9 781949 140132